disquiet

ALSO BY ZÜLFÜ LIVANELI

Serenade for Nadia

Bliss

disquiet

ZÜLFÜ LIVANELI

TRANSLATED FROM THE TURKISH
BY BRENDAN FREELY

Other Press / New York

Production editor: Yvonne E. Cárdenas
Text designer: Jennifer Daddio / Bookmark Design & Media Inc.
This book was set in Cochin and Charme by
Alpha Design & Composition of Pittsfield NH.

1 3 5 7 9 10 8 6 4 2

For information write to Other Press LLC,
267 Fifth Avenue, 6th Floor, New York, NY 10016.
Or visit our Web site: www.otherpress.com

Library of Congress Cataloging-in-Publication Data
Names: Livaneli, Zülfü, 1946- author. | Freely, Brendan 1959- translator.
Title: Disquiet : a novel / Zülfü Livaneli ; translated from the Turkish
by Brendan Freely.
Other titles: Huzursuzluk. English
Description: New York : Other Press, 2021.
Identifiers: LCCN 2020043408 (print) | LCCN 2020043409 (ebook) |
ISBN 9781635420326 (paperback) | ISBN 9781635420333 (ebook)
Subjects: LCSH: Yezidis—Fiction. | IS (Organization)—Fiction. |
Syria—History—Civil War, 2011—Refugees—Fiction. | War stories. |
Romance fiction.
Classification: LCC PL248.L58 H8913 2021 (print) | LCC PL248.L58 (ebook) |
DDC 894/.3533—dc23
LC record available at https://lccn.loc.gov/2020043408
LC ebook record available at https://lccn.loc.gov/2020043409

To Ülker and Aylin

With gratitude to my dear friend,

NECATI YAĞCI

for expanding my knowledge on Mardin

While my son was dying
The flowers were screaming and budding.

—ANONYMOUS ANATOLIAN MOTHER

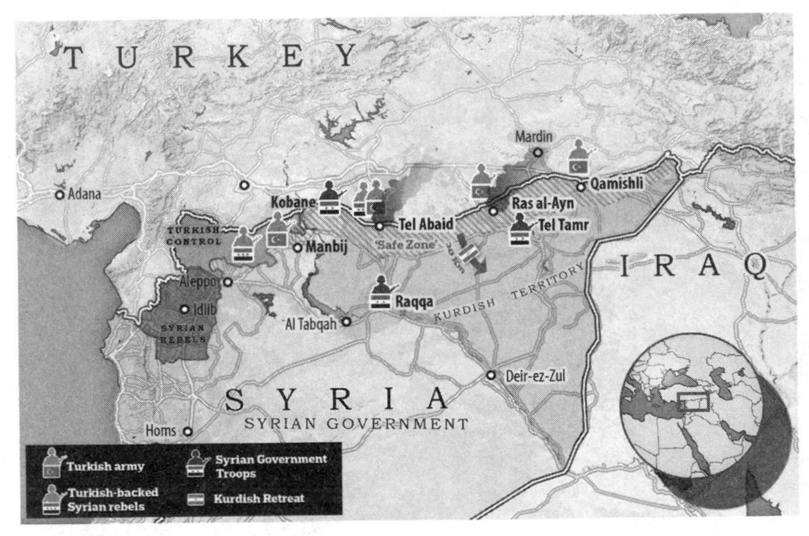

Turkey–Syria Border, October 2019

AUTHOR'S NOTE

The ancient town of Mardin, where *Disquiet* takes place, is right on the Turkey-Syria border. This part of Turkey has little in common with the Aegean, Black Sea, Caucasus, or Mediterranean regions. Mardin is part of Mesopotamia, not far from the Iraqi and Syrian borders, where Kurdish fighters, especially the YPG (the primary militia of the Syrian Democratic Forces), regularly clash with the Turkish Army and where more than fifty thousand people have been killed since 1978. With American and Russian armies involved there as well, this area has become one of the most volatile spots in the world. Our protagonist is a young Yezidi (like Nobel Peace Prize laureate Nadia Murad). Yezidis practice a religion that is unique and that precedes Christianity. For centuries, Yezidi have been massacred by Arabs, Ottoman rulers, and others—and more recently, by ISIS.

Turkey isn't a single entity. There are, so to speak, many countries within Turkey, where many different languages are spoken. Turkey has split allegiances. Turks from the westernmost cities, such Istanbul, İzmir, or Bursa, have trouble identifying the languages, traditions, and cultures of Mesopotamia. Ibrahim, the male protagonist of *Disquiet*, who is from there, thinks that he is proud of his roots, but in fact his attachment is purely romantic and not based on true understanding. His alienation from a culture he would love to embrace is a crucial part of the novel, and is representative of the fact that a majority of Turkish people rarely visit the eastern border of their land, nor can they read Arabic. The culture they identify with the most is Greek, since Greeks and Turks lived together for five hundred years as subjects of the Ottoman Empire.

disquiet

Do you know what harese *is, my son? It's an old Arabic word. The words for determination, greed, and craving are derived from it. I'll tell you what* harese *is, my boy. You know how they call camels the ships of the desert? These blessed animals can walk and walk through the desert without eating or drinking for three weeks, thirsty and hungry; I mean that's how tough they are. But there's a thistle in the desert they're very fond of. Wherever they see this thistle, they bite some off and begin chewing. The sharp thistle lacerates the camel's mouth, and these cuts begin to bleed. The camel likes it even more when the salty taste of the blood mixes with the thistle. So the more it eats the more it bleeds, and the more it bleeds the more it eats. Somehow it can't get its fill of its own blood, and if it's not stopped, the camel will bleed to death. This is called* harese. *As I said earlier, the words for determination, greed, and craving come from it. This is the custom throughout the Middle East, my son. Throughout history people have killed one another without ever realizing that they are actually killing themselves. They become intoxicated by the taste of their own blood.*

journey
to
hussein

THAT WHICH MIXES WITH THE RED WIND

What made it difficult for me to tell this story were two statements that I heard and was unable to forget. They kept wandering through my mind.

The first was "You can't protect me any longer, Mother, not even if you took me and put me back in your womb." The second was "I was a human being." Two different people, two different places, and two different statements that affected me deeply.

But first let me tell you how it all began. We were gathered around the oval table on the second floor of the newspaper for the editorial meeting we held every morning at 11:00. We were going over the news, and the chief of each section was filling us in on the details. As usual, the colleague we'd nicknamed "Chief Inspector Recep" was laying out his most gruesome photographs for the news that would appear on page three. We were accustomed to the way he spoke: whenever he said he'd got a fantastic shot, we knew we would be confronted by images of horrifying accidents or murders and that we would definitely see mangled bodies. In the language of journalism, the more blood in a photograph the more fantastic it is. He began with the femicides that he referred to as "common occurrences." A young woman who was stabbed in the street by her former husband, a policeman who shot his wife with his service revolver and then killed himself. He read each story, showed the photographs, and then moved on.

In the end he spoke of an incident to which he didn't attach much importance. A Turk named Hussein Yılmaz, who worked at his two older brothers' pizza place in the German city of Duisburg, had been stabbed and killed by neo-Nazis. The severely wounded thirty-two-year-old native of Mardin had been brought to the hospital but did not survive. The mayor of the city made a statement deploring the incident and defending the rights of the millions of Turks living in Germany. He went on to say how they couldn't allow this kind of hostility toward Islam and Turks. There was no gruesome photograph because they don't print photographs like that in Germany, but a stringer had found a photograph of the deceased in the Mardin census records.

The editor decided to go with a brief version of the story, since it might catch the interest of religious readers, but something else had occurred to me. If this person's name was Hussein Yılmaz, and if he'd been born in

Mardin and was thirty-two years old, it couldn't be anyone other than my childhood friend Hussein, unless two people named Hussein Yılmaz were born in the same city in the same year.

I asked Chief Inspector Recep where in Mardin this person was born, and when he answered that his official residence was in the Kızıltepe district and that he'd been born there, I had not the slightest doubt that the man killed in Germany was our Hussein. The boy I'd sat next to in class for years, with whom I'd played tipcat and marbles and stolen baby birds from their nests, that small, curious boy I hadn't seen in years.

When I flew to meet Hussein's family in Mardin, that ancient city, lost in time on the Syrian border, was once again covered with red dust. The streets and the clouds of red dust that painted the houses seemed like a set designed by an expert director, appropriate for creating the atmosphere for the burning pain of a family that had lost a son and for the prophetic words Hussein had uttered to his mother.

I was familiar with these clouds of red dust. As a child, when Hussein and I were at school together, red winds like this would also blow in from the Syrian desert, and we would all be covered in red in a desert heat that made it difficult to even breathe. When the red wind came, the shopkeepers would gather their goods off the counters. Everyone would rush inside, and those who remained outside ran along coughing as they held handkerchiefs over their mouths. When I returned to my city after many years, I was once again greeted by the same red clouds.

"You can't protect me any longer, Mother, not even if you took me and put me back in your womb!"

These had been his last words to his mother. The old woman, whose eyes were red from weeping, kept repeating these words as she wiped her tears with the edge of her white muslin headscarf. His sister, Aysel, had heard this too. She'd also been there when they were saying farewell at the door. She'd thrown her arms around her older brother's neck, but he'd sunk into a deep listlessness. It was as if he'd given up on life: he didn't even raise his arms. In any event he couldn't raise his left arm because of the bullet wound in his shoulder. It was as if he knew he was going to his death; his sister said it was then that she felt there was nothing they could do to help him, and that perhaps it was because of that girl.

"You can't protect me any longer, Mother, not even if you took me and put me back in your womb!"

These weren't the last words he uttered in his life, but it was the last thing he said when he was parting from his mother and his sister. In any event his father had already died, and his two older brothers were in Germany.

The day Hussein bade farewell to his family was also tinted red like this. Aysel told me that when she last saw her older brother at the door, his face was orange from the dust. Her mother poured a bucket of water after him, calling after him to not think bad thoughts and to go and return like water, but he'd already disappeared into that red cloud.

"The last time I saw my son he looked as if his face was covered in blood," his mother said. Then she turned to Aysel: "Don't ever mention that she-devil's name in this house again. She consumed my mighty son, she brought disaster wherever she went, she extinguished our hearth—that she-devil should only be referred to as a she-devil."

About two months after he left Mardin, Hussein was in the emergency room of a hospital in Germany. It was there he spoke his last words, which he struggled to get out: "I was a human being." According to his older brother, when the Indian doctor heard Hussein repeat these words before he died, he'd recorded it on his telephone because he realized that no one present could understand. Later, the doctor played the recording for Hussein's brothers, and asked what it meant. They translated it into German for him. The doctor, who must have thought they'd mistranslated, asked if he'd said "I'm a human being."

"No," they said, "he said 'I was a human being.' He's using the past tense and talking as if he's already dead."

The medical report his older brother brought back to Mardin with his remains read "Hussein Yılmaz, citizen of the Republic of Turkey, thirty-two years old, died on September 26, 2016, at 11:44 p.m., as a result of knife wounds to the abdomen and kidneys."

As soon as I got to Mardin, I saw the vacant lot where nobody played tipcat anymore, though somehow it was still empty and had remained safe from rapacious developers. Hussein suddenly entered my mind from that other world called childhood. I imagined myself playing tipcat, holding a stick, hitting a piece of wood balanced loosely on a rock and causing it to fly into the air, watching it spin in the air, then hitting it again to send it flying into the distance. Later I would describe this game as poor man's baseball—the memory was so vivid that I could feel the stick in my hands, and it brought me back to the past. This surprised me.

The old me had returned. I could picture not just Hussein, but our other friends as well: Mehmet, Raif, Safter, Fikret, Münir, Tahir. The smallest and thinnest of us was sharp-faced Hussein. He didn't (couldn't) arm wrestle with any of us because from the beginning he accepted he would lose. To make up for this, he was the best student in the Koran course we were all sent to. When we entered the dilapidated room in which the course was given, took the little Arabic alphabet books from the amulets around our necks, placed them on the lecterns, and knelt on the floor, he would start reciting fluently and without effort the letters the rest of us found so difficult: "Alif, beh, teh, seh, jeem..."

He would surprise us by what he said: for instance, that he wanted to see the Prophet's face for one second and then die immediately afterward. In any event his mind was always full of thoughts about death. He kept saying that the red winds blew as a sign that the Day of Judgment was coming, that it was a warning for us not to get caught up in the blessings of this ephemeral world. We would laugh when he said this, as the desert sand filled our mouths and worked its way between our teeth, using whatever we could find to cover our faces as we rushed to get home as soon as possible. When we hunted birds with our slingshots he would reproach us for sinning. "Don't you eat chicken, man?" we would tease him. "That's a bird, these are birds; what difference does it make if it's on the ground or in the air?"

"Nooooo," he would say, shaking his head thoughtfully, "maybe these birds are descended from the swifts who attacked the idolater Abraha's army as it marched toward Mecca on elephants, the ones who destroyed it by dropping stones from their beaks, how do you know that's not true?"

Ismail, the toughest of us, would make a show of spitting on the ground. Then he'd say fuck off, fuck off, Hussein, you've ruined everything, if you're going to do that why don't you just stay home, man. Don't spoil our fun.

At school one day our teacher Cemal, whom we called Squeaky because he was constantly polishing his wire-framed glasses, told us what a fatwa is. He asked if one of us had to issue a fatwa, who would be worthy of the task. He laughed when we all turned toward Hussein. "Yes," he said, "in this class Hussein is most suited if a fatwa has to be issued. This boy is going to be a mullah when he grows up."

The days lasted longer, the sun set later, time flowed more slowly. We writhed with boredom because we didn't know what to do. We tried to invent games to play, we sat and drew in the sand with our sticks in the blistering heat until our heads began to spin, we rolled hoops, we competed with each other in spinning tops.

I received the impression from this world as if it had happened to someone else, as if the "me" who hurried from plaza to plaza in Istanbul, rushing breathlessly to catch the bus or the metro, was under the influence of a dream he'd had. Which of these two selves was the dominant, that self or this self? *That* me was the shy, frightened child who waved to his headscarfed mother and hajji father from the back of the bus that was taking him to school in the big city. It seemed as if since arriving in Mardin the other I, my earlier self, was reasserting itself. The painful pleasure of peeling off the brown scabs on our knees to reveal the pink, running flesh beneath; how at the hammam our mothers would get soap in our eyes when they poured basins of boiling water over our heads; the parts that hurt most when we were scrubbed with the coarse bath glove, our underarms and our lower backs; the heavy smell that came from the section that was closed off with red-and-pink striped breechcloth—the section that children were not to approach (we didn't know then that the women were using depilatory herbs); the stationary columns of light that came in through the windows of the hammam's dome, and the tiny particles that danced slowly within them. In short, my body was remembering the land of childhood more quickly than my mind: it was filling me like slowly rising water.

I was having trouble picturing Hussein as a grown man. It was as if they'd shot that scrawny boy in Mardin, and my small, innocent-faced classmate had been stabbed to death in Germany.

Apart from facial expressions that remained from childhood, the young man in the photograph that had come to the newspaper and the photographs in the family album was someone completely different. He wore round, wire-framed glasses, his hair was thinning, he had a narrow face and thin lips, and everything about him said that he was a timid young man. There was nothing memorable about him. When his mother—whom in those days we called Aunt Adviye: she'd seemed old to us then, but now this woman of the East walked with her back bent, and there were deep lines on her face—gave me the old album, she told me not to forget to bring it back, because it was all she had left of her son.

I asked if that girl's picture was in the album. She waved her hand vehemently and said no, there was no picture of that devil: "There had been a picture, but to keep it from bringing more evil to this house I first cut the eyes out with scissors, then recited a prayer as I burned it in the stove. And to keep her spirit from ever coming back I hung wild rue on the walls and spread romaine lettuce everywhere."

Ever since I'd entered that old two-story house something had been making me uneasy, but I didn't understand what it was. Now it sprang into my consciousness like cold wind through an open window. As Aunt Adviye had said, there was romaine lettuce all over the house. There were fresh green leaves of romaine on the television, on the sofa, on the coffee tables, on the armchairs. Dozens of romaine lettuce leaves behind the doors, behind the main door, on the balcony and indeed even in the courtyard. Even if the woman hadn't lost her mind from the pain of losing her son, this display of romaine was enough to make visitors lose their minds. I was about to ask her about it when she took down a silk-covered Koran that was hanging on the wall, kissed it three times and put it to her head. Aysel raised her eyebrows to keep me quiet and gestured that she would explain later, so I held my tongue. I left and went to the hotel holding the photo album and thinking about romaine lettuce. I was almost certain that when I saw Aysel later she would tell me that the poor woman had lost her mind, but that's not what happened. She looked at me with those dark almond eyes that I hadn't been able to stop looking at when I was a child and said that the romaine lettuce had a meaning: the girl was afraid of it.

"She's afraid of romaine, of ordinary romaine?"

"Yes, yes. In fact everything came out into the open because of the romaine."

I asked her what had come out into the open, and she answered that the girl named Meleknaz was a devil.

"How is there any connection between romaine lettuce and the devil..."

"There is one, but we didn't know about it. We were just as surprised as you are."

Since I didn't think that Aysel and her mother had both lost their minds at the same time, there was a real mystery behind the leaves of romaine that had been hung everywhere. I was becoming increasingly drawn into the story, but I didn't know how I was going to connect so many disparate elements and incidents. The girl they called a devil, my childhood friend Hussein who was in love with her, his having been shot in Mardin, his death in Germany, and now this romaine in the house. Especially the romaine.

"This girl named Meleknaz, the one you call a devil, was she Hussein's wife?" I asked Aysel.

"They were in the process of getting married, but there were problems because the girl was a Syrian refugee. They were dealing with that."

"Meleknaz? Is she Syrian?" I asked as I tried to clarify things.

"Yes," Aysel said, "in fact they met at the refugee camp. He didn't know it was going to cost him his life when he fell madly . . ."

Aysel stopped speaking. She trembled slightly and made a soft sobbing sound. I completed her sentence, saying he'd fallen in love with her.

"No," she said with rising defiance, "is it possible to fall in love with a demon? That girl addled his wits, who knows what spells she put on him, she got him to leave his former fiancée and stand against his own family."

"Come on, Aysel," I said. "Everything you say confuses me even more. Can't you just tell me the whole story from start to finish?"

"No," she said, "I can't do that now, my brother's remains are arriving tomorrow, and we're going to bury him. I'm in a lot of pain, and there are a thousand things I have to do."

She gave me a last glance with those almond eyes that I still looked at in admiration, then left me alone with my confused mood and my increasingly perplexing questions.

In the evening I left the hotel and walked the narrow streets between the stone buildings of this ancient city, past the workshops where Assyrian masters made silver filigree. Then I walked some distance out of the city and climbed the hill to the Kasımiye madrassa, as I used to do when I was a child.

From here the entire plain was at my feet; it made you feel as if you could see all of Mesopotamia. The sun was setting directly across from Mardin castle, painting the stone houses red. It was a place where time had stopped, and frozen within it were Crusaders, Tamerlane's Mongols, Artuqids, Seljuks, Assyrians, Armenians, Arabs, and Kurds. Boarding a plane in Istanbul and in two hours going back thousands of years and diving into the history of Mesopotamia gave me a feeling similar to melancholy, but it wasn't melancholy. I don't know whether to call it confusion or yearning, but I was seized by a complicated feeling that I couldn't quite put my finger on. My tumultuous life in Istanbul, the wife from whom I'd recently separated, the difficulties of getting divorced, the excitement of working at the newspaper, my desk and my computer all seemed far away. Just across from me was the Syrian border and the district of Qamishli.

The day was ending. The evening call to prayer came first from the Great Mosque and then from the other mosques, and I felt a shiver within me. I had childhood memories of the Great Mosque as well. On religious holidays we would be woken early and be taken there for prayers after performing ablutions in the fountain. That beautiful mosque was built by a Christian architect, in this city where so many faiths mix together.

As the sky grew dark, a murkiness descended, and when the details of the great plain were erased it began to resemble a vast ocean. I felt as if I were looking at an endless sea. I felt as if I was about to cry, but I didn't know what it was that made me feel like this. I remembered an old Arabic poem my grandfather taught me: "Noble people possess a melancholy even in their most cheerful moments, and as for lesser souls, they're cheerful even when they're most miserable." A poem suited for a cheerless and unpleasant life. A time when people seldom laughed, women and children spoke in hushed tones when the men were home, the radio playing Arabic songs was shut off as soon as Father and Grandfather came home, and family meals were eaten hurriedly and in silence.

As I left the Kasımiye madrassa, which had been built by Artuqid sultans, I realized what was causing my melancholy: loneliness. I was alone in this city; I had no family here. Those who were still alive had moved to Ankara or Izmir, and I no longer had any relationship with them. I no longer had any family ties: my grandfather and my parents were in the cemetery. This was no longer my city. Thousand-year-old buildings with cinder block extensions and extra floors, tangled electric and telephone wires that looked like spilled intestines—the ugliness that the darkness was concealing.

Faint lights were coming on in the houses. It was as if all the anguish of Mesopotamia had descended on the city with the darkness. I realized that I badly needed a drink—I wasn't hungry but I wanted to drink. From what I'd read, it was difficult to find alcohol in the city now. They didn't serve alcohol at the hotel or in any of the restaurants. Even though this place was famous for its mahaleb-flavored Assyrian wine and the home of the *reyhanî* dances, in which one dancer swayed slowly and descended first on one knee, and then the other, to the rhythm of the music, while balancing a glass of raki on his forehead without spilling a drop.

When I was a child, Islam in Mardin was something different. It was a tender world. When we interrupted a grandmother's prayers, or climbed on her back when she was prostrating herself, the poor woman, fearing her prayers would be spoiled, would do nothing more than repeat the words more loudly in gentle protest. When the children insisted on fasting during Ramadan, the adults would say fine, fast for three days, one day at the beginning, one in the middle and one at the end, then add a zero and it will be thirty. Despite our insistence, we couldn't wait for the breaking of the fast: we would secretly drink water and eat food we'd purloined from the kitchen. They never chided us for this, and indeed at the table they would ask God to accept our sacrifice.

Those were the festive days when Assyrians, Muslims, and Zoroastrians, including Parsis, mingled in the marketplace and at school and celebrated one another's holy days... But now the atmosphere was closed, the city had been darkened by the shadow of a sterner, angrier Islam.

When my former self walked the streets of this city holding his father's hand, he was almost overwhelmed by the smell of grilling meat and anise that wafted from some of the restaurants. This was such a pleasant and distinctive smell, a different realm from the food we ate at home. People drank raki and mahaleb-flavored Assyrian wine at home too, but the heady smell of the mixture of kebabs and raki that drifted from the restaurants was something else. Now as I walk the streets they seem darker, less cheerful, more deserted. This was a city living in fear, caught in the middle of the conflicts between ISIS, the PKK, and the state security forces.

The distant sounds of gunfire and barking dogs rang in my ears. To escape the indescribable feeling of loss that the city evoked in me, I headed for the Cercis Murat Mansion, which was famous even as far away as Istanbul. I think this was the only restaurant in Mardin that still served alcohol, and perhaps this was because the owner was a woman. The restaurant in this magnificent stone mansion was deserted, with most of the tables empty; tourists didn't come any more, and the locals were afraid to leave their houses. I ordered mahaleb-flavored Assyrian wine and chose lamb shank with quince from the menu. They used to tell us that the mansion once belonged to the Armenian Tüfekçiyan family. After the deportations, it was taken over by the Assyrian Cercis Murat...in any event a lot of Armenian property was shared out among the people of Mardin.

The wine was thick and slightly acrid, but the mahaleb left a pleasant aftertaste. I asked the waiter whether they sold the wine by the bottle. I intended to buy two bottles to bring back to the hotel, since even if I couldn't drink in the lobby I supposed I could drink in my room. He told me they didn't, but that the Assyrian jewelers in the center of town sold it: they made it at home.

I thought about who might be able to fill me in on Hussein's adventure. I didn't suppose it would be difficult to find my old friends. Who would talk to me, who would tell me the truth? And did any of them really know what was true and what was a lie? If they also believed that the refugee girl Meleknaz was a devil, they wouldn't tell me anything. Who shot Hussein here, why did they shoot him, how did they shoot him, and how was it that despite receiving two bullet wounds here, he died later, in Germany?

Fortunately, my mind was slightly clouded as I walked back along the narrow stone streets to my hotel, which had been converted from the Zinciriye madrassa, or these questions would have kept me awake. That night, a girl with a devil's tail entered my dreams.

AWAKE, HUSSEIN, FROM YOUR DEEP SLUMBER

Hussein's older brother, Salim, had brought his remains by plane to Istanbul and then to Mardin, and as he was lowered into the ground, women, professional mourners, were beating their chests and pulling their hair, letting out heartrending screams and telling his family how manly, brave, handsome, and unfortunate he'd been, bringing more tears to their eyes. I knew these black-clad professional mourners; they were at every funeral and they earned every penny they made—so much so that a passerby might think that they were the ones who were really burning with anguish, that they were suffering more deeply than the relatives and friends.

They shouted in Arabic, Turkish, and Kurdish, "Rise, Hussein, rise, what is this slumber, this deep slumber, your horse remains tethered in the stable, your sheep have been left untended, let mourning remain far from us, rise, Hussein, rise, what is this slumber?"

As they shouted they beat their clasped hands in a rhythmic manner against their hearts, heads, and chests. They had purple tattoos on their hands and faces, and most of them also had their lower lips tattooed purple. They believed that a slave had once bit the Prophet's daughter, Fatima, and that her lower lip had been bruised, so they tattooed their lower lips purple.

My grandmother had a gazelle tattooed on her chest; I asked her once why she'd done this, and she replied that when she was distressed she wanted to see gazelles racing across her chest. Did it hurt, I asked, and she replied that it had hurt a lot, it bled and stung, it peeled off seven times and then it turned purple like this. The women who made these tattoos would take milk from a mother who was suckling a baby girl—for whatever reason it didn't work if the mother had given birth to a boy—mixed it with soot, then dipped three needles into it in order to make the tattoo. I saw that my Assyrian classmate Emmanuel had a crucifix tattooed on his arm. When I asked him why he did something so painful and gory, he said, "We do this for our religion, but we don't stain our faces."

My grandmother was buried in this gloomy cemetery, and so was my grandfather, my father, and my mother. Their undutiful son had visited their untended graves, covered in yellowing weeds, the morning before Hussein's funeral. He stood by their graves for five or six minutes, feeling strange and not knowing what to do. He read the names and dates on the gravestones over and over again; his mother and father weren't here, he thought, they're gone. So, then, what is there here, just their bones? He'd heard that the Greeks take the bones of their loved ones out of their graves after three years and then store the bones at home. That meant that after three years there was nothing but bones left. He wondered if he should take his parents' bones to Istanbul. He could look at them every day, but would they forgive him his mistakes, the insensitivity with which he'd abandoned his family, the crudeness with which he'd belittled Mardin and his own people? Of course he couldn't do anything like that. At least not from his parents' perspective. Unlike their "Westernized" son, they were Eastern to their marrow, and even though their marrow was gone now, at least their bones and their memories belonged to Mesopotamia.

I went up to a tall, mustachioed man in the crowd and whispered that I hadn't known professional mourners still existed. The man looked me over, then said that this was an old custom; nowadays some people still call them and some people don't. Then he turned his attention back to the funeral. It was clear he thought I was a curious visitor.

"We had professional mourners when my grandfather was buried here, Mehmet," I said.

At this he turned his head and looked at me carefully. He looked me up and down curiously; he was trying to place who I was. Then his face lit up.

"Ibrahim?" he asked, "Ibrahim?"

"Yes, Mehmet," I whispered, "I'm Ibrahim."

To avoid being disrespectful, we didn't shake hands or embrace, we just touched hands as we stood solemnly side by side. Just then we saw Aysel, who had cut off the two waist-length braids that she clearly hadn't touched since childhood, throw herself on her older brother's grave.

A GUEST FROM LALISH VALLEY

"I'm astounded," said Mehmet, "I'm really surprised, Ibrahim, after all these years, I hear nothing of you for so long and then you suddenly just appear next to me, and at Hussein's funeral. You know, Hussein and I used to talk about you, we wondered where you were and what you were doing... We were curious about you, you were so far from us. We got stuck in this city, Ibrahim, it never even occurred to us to go anywhere else. We carried on the lives our fathers and grandfathers lived, but meanwhile, as you can see, the city changed, Mardin changed, maybe we changed too, who knows.

"As for our old friends, Raif died in a traffic accident, Muharrem got cancer but he recovered, he runs a car agency, and as for Hussein... They founded a university here, did you know that? Hussein, he was always the best student among us, graduated from their medical school. Maybe you remember how much he liked to help people, how softhearted he was. Yes, as you said, he even felt sorry for the birds we hunted, I'd forgotten about that. That never changed, indeed as he got older he became even more compassionate. We're all compassionate people, but no one could be as compassionate as he was. He devoted his life to the poor, the sick, and the oppressed, and he wasn't just kind to people but to all creatures. Do you remember the donkeys that used to carry loads to the upper neighborhood, those donkeys they used on those steep streets that were too narrow for cars? Not long ago the municipality made them part of the permanent staff, can you believe that? The donkeys became part of the staff, but this didn't change anything about the lives of these sick, weak, and weary creatures. He took time out from his busy schedule to take care of these donkeys. As he put balm on their wounds and treated their illnesses he spoke to them with such tenderness; the donkeys would nod their heads as if they understood him. Hussein even told us about a donkey that wept in gratitude. Get out of here, we said, we thought he was exaggerating, has anyone ever seen a donkey cry? In his usual ingenuous manner he swore that it was true, he insisted that the donkey had actually cried. What a guy he was, who could have guessed his life would end this way. Yes, as you said, we should have a drink together in his honor, let's have a drink to honor the most kindhearted person in the world.

"They say compassion can bring affliction, you know, too much of anything is too much. Hussein was extreme. If he hadn't rushed to the refugee camps, none of this would have happened to him. But he couldn't stop himself, he felt deeply sorry for the refugees who were flooding in from Syria. He kept insisting that he was going to help them.

"There are thousands of Syrian refugees here, you know, they live in tent cities, their lives are really hard, how could poor Hussein heal thousands of people? Yet he still did everything he could, he leaned over backward and he wore himself out. If it wasn't for his compassion he wouldn't have had any problems in life. He had a home and a job, he was engaged to be married, he was counting the days to his wedding.

"What, you didn't hear that he was engaged? I'm not talking about the she-devil; his fiancée's a local girl, from a wealthy family: her name is Safiye. You must be talking about the other girl, the one he met in the refugee camp. Sure, I'll tell you the whole story, or at least as much of it as I know. We didn't know what was happening to him—he became stranger and stranger as he went back and forth to the refugee camps. There's this organization called Doctors Without Borders, doctors come from France and so forth: apparently they help the refugees. Hussein started going around with them; he treated women and children who were sick or wounded. Of course, the refugees were cold in winter, do you know how many people burned to death because they lit stoves in those tents!

"This Syria business was really bad. So many miserable people had to take to the roads to flee death, but they didn't find any comfort when they arrived here. Yes, you're right, most of them fled ISIS, but there were also people who fled the government forces or Al Nusra. All of them were in a desperate situation, but it was the Yezidis who faced the worst persecution. ISIS raided their villages. They beheaded all males over the age of ten, took the women and girls prisoner and raped them, and then later they sold them. The boys under ten were trained to be ISIS militants.

"Those who were able to escape the massacre took shelter in Lalish. Lalish is a sacred place for them, they've always fled there in times of persecution. ISIS pursued them there too, but when the Kurds came to the Yezidis' defense they retreated.

"Of course all of this relates to Hussein, otherwise I wouldn't have gone into so much detail. During his last months here he was going to the Yezidi camps. The Yezidis almost became an obsession with him, because they'd been oppressed and persecuted the most. He talked about them all the time—how they'd been marginalized by every other religious group, and how in recent times they'd seen the worst persecution from ISIS. According to ISIS, spilling Yezidi blood was permissible, indeed those who killed Yezidis went to heaven. Why? I don't know too much, but a few people I asked said the Yezidis worshipped Satan. Who the hell would worship Satan? But I suppose there are people who do.

"In fact my father knows about them, do you remember my father? Yes, yes, thankfully he's still alive, he just turned eighty. He's in good health, he's as tough as leather, thank God. He can't read as much as he used to because his eyesight is failing, but his mind is still sharp. Exactly, you're right, you remembered, he used to tutor Hussein in religion after school. It's been so long I'd forgotten about that, you've got a good memory.

"Hussein met this girl called Meleknaz in the Yezidi camp. I never saw her, but those who did said she was no great beauty; they said she was a dark, skinny girl. They didn't understand what Hussein saw in her, but the heart wants what the heart wants . . . Hussein left his fiancée for that girl, and poor Safiye cried her eyes out. She kept on about how witchcraft could be the only reason he'd leave a beautiful, wealthy fiancée like she was and fall desperately in love with that miserable girl, and people agreed with her.

"To tell the truth, I thought the same thing. What Hussein did doesn't make any sense. On top of that, the girl had a baby, a baby who had been born blind. We were never able to find out whether it was the result of rape or if she'd been married. I suppose Hussein lost his wits when he saw this thin girl holding a blind baby in one of those tents. He was determined to restore the child's sight: he consulted the French doctors, but as far as I heard they weren't able to help. The girl had no one else in the world except that baby. Hussein applied to get permission to marry her, and indeed they performed a traditional Yezidi engagement ceremony in the tent. Of course we didn't know any of this then, and his family didn't know either. Anyway, these are all rumors, no one knows the real story; there are some who say that among the Yezidi, marrying a Muslim is forbidden, I don't know. And maybe they just made an agreement between themselves. However he did it, he managed to get permission to take the girl out of the camp. He brought her straight to his mother's house. All he said was that this was his new fiancée and that her name was Meleknaz. His mother fainted and collapsed on the floor. I suppose it was because she liked Safiye so much, you know the two families are distantly related. When she came to, his mother asked him how he was ever going to look anyone in the face again. 'You have such a beautiful fiancée, where did this dark girl come from?'

"The Yezidi girl standing by the door with the baby in her arms—at the time they didn't know she was Yezidi, she didn't know Turkish so she didn't understand what they were saying, but she must have sensed what was going on from their attitude. So she turned and began to leave. Hussein went and took her by the arm and dragged her in. 'Mother,' he said, 'if I'm your son, then this is your daughter-in-law, it would be best if you accepted this at once, or else I'm packing up and leaving.'

"Aysel said she'd never seen her softhearted brother behave so firmly. At first they thought he'd gone mad, but later on when they looked back over what had happened, they realized that the devil had been playing games with him. 'What could my poor brother do?' said Aysel. 'His wits had been addled by that devil's black magic.' After Hussein stood up to her like that, Aunt Adviye didn't say anything more, of course. She welcomed the girl in, and the girl came very reluctantly. According to Aysel, that minx put on such airs. She acted as if she was doing them a favor: she didn't even look at us, she didn't smile, she just stood there like a wild animal.

"If it had been up to them, they would never have pitied this snooty girl, but when Aysel took the baby in her arms—and she had to insist because the girl wouldn't give her the baby and looked as if she might lash out, Meleknaz only did so after Hussein stroked her shoulder and said something into her ear—she saw that the baby was blind. She told me that it was as if the baby's eyes were covered by white clouds. She was such a beautiful girl, but she was unlucky, very unlucky. Just then, for a moment, she wondered if this was Hussein's baby, but she immediately dismissed the thought. Hussein had only met the girl recently, there was no knowing who the father was, but he was probably Syrian. Aysel tried to give her mother the baby, but her mother wouldn't take her. If she hadn't been afraid of losing her son she would have been wise enough to eject her from the house, but she didn't, but she wasn't very welcoming either. What a strange business, isn't it?

"Yes, yes, of course I saw Hussein. I spoke to him, I tried to talk him out of it, but the Hussein we knew was gone, he'd been replaced by this stern, quiet man. I told him that he was hurting everyone, his mother, Aysel, and most of all his fiancée Safiye. She didn't deserve this, but nothing I said had any impact on him. He just stared straight ahead.

"'If that's how it is,' I said, 'tell me about her, who is this girl, where did you find her?' He said he'd met her in the refugee camp, she'd fled from Syria, and she had a blind baby. 'It's clear you pity the poor girl,' I said, 'I know how softhearted you are, and it's obvious that this tears you apart. Fine, but you can't marry everyone you feel sorry for. Help her, get treatment for her child, do whatever you want, but what the hell are you doing, Hussein, what are you doing? Is it worth abandoning your fiancée and being estranged from your family? I feel really bad about the refugees too, those poor people have been driven out of their homes, they're living in tents, but what can you do, you can't save everyone, and since you're particularly concerned about this girl then do as I said, help her, in fact let's all help her, let all Muslim believers help this girl and her fatherless child.'

"When I said this he raised his head and gave me a long look. There was such hopelessness in his eyes, it would be a lie if I said I didn't pity him. Of course at the time I didn't know why he was looking at me like that because he hadn't told me. When I made my remark about Muslims, a look of great pain settled on his face. 'What's going on, Hussein,' I asked, 'why are you looking at me as if you're about to cry? Is it such a bad idea, that we all pitch in and save the girl?' We were in my shop, we were drinking tea.

"As soon as I said this Hussein stood up. 'You can't save her, Mehmet,' he said, 'don't waste your time trying, you can't save her, I asked if he thought we were that uncharitable, and he said no, there was something else. I asked him what it was but he wouldn't say. I insisted but he wouldn't say a word. Then he went, leaving me full of questions. Anyway, I never got the chance to see Hussein again.

"Of course I'm saddened, but I'm also going mad with curiosity. We'd been friends since childhood but there was a secret between us, there were things he was keeping from me. Two days later I learned about the situation from Aysel. I called out to her as she was passing the shop; I asked her if she had a moment to talk. That's when she told me. I felt as if I'd been shot in the head.

"According to Aysel, a day or two after Hussein brought the girl, his mother softened a bit. She had to, what could the poor woman do. She was helpless, but she tried to console herself. 'Let's give it some time,' she said to her daughter, 'maybe he'll come to his senses. We can go to Sister Tevhide to break the spell. We'll take him to one of the hodjas whose prayers get answered; perhaps my boy was cursed or attacked by djinnis.' How could those poor women have known that this was actually the case? They thought he'd brought home a Muslim Arab girl. Anyway, the girl started helping them out in the kitchen and so forth. She never spoke, but one time they heard her singing a lullaby to the baby in her room but they couldn't figure out what language she was singing in—it was neither Arabic nor Kurdish. Meanwhile Hussein went to Safiye to break their engagement. They fought. Safiye shouted and hollered at Hussein. She said he'd destroyed her honor, and then she took off her engagement ring and threw it in his face, but this didn't even bother him.

"If I drink any more I'm going to pass out right here, but I wouldn't be able to talk about these things without drinking. What you're going to hear next is going to surprise you even more, come on, let's drink to Hussein.

"Of course, curious relatives started dropping by Aunt Adviye's house. Some of them were pleased, some of them were truly upset, but they were all like, what's going on, why is she behaving like this? And just as they were talking about how standoffish the bride-to-be was, didn't the girl's deceit come out into the open! Now, this is strange. Aunt Adviye, Aysel, and Meleknaz were preparing food in the kitchen. The guests were waiting, they had to serve the food. Aysel took some romaine lettuce out of the fridge and started chopping it for the salad. Just then the girl went crazy, she screamed and raced out. She didn't just flee the kitchen, she fled the house, barefoot and with her head uncovered, forgetting all about her baby. Mother and daughter had no idea what had happened; they were flabbergasted. As they stood there in amazement, wondering why the girl had suddenly gone mad, the guests came into the kitchen. 'What happened,' they asked, 'the girl screamed and ran out of here as if she'd seen the devil, did you have an argument?' 'No, really,' said Aysel, 'I swear nothing happened, she was preparing the pastry and I was making the salad, she just suddenly lost it.'

"As everyone was shaking their heads and looking at each other in confusion, Hussein's uncle looked around the kitchen, and he saw the romaine Aysel had been chopping. 'Was this what you were chopping,' he asked. And she said, 'Yes, Uncle, I'd just taken it out of the fridge and was beginning to chop it...'

"When he heard this her uncle closed his eyes. After muttering 'I take refuge in God from the cursed Satan,' he said, 'Look, this girl is a Yezidi.' 'Good God,' everyone cried. And everyone repeated 'I take refuge in God from the accursed Satan,' and started reciting the opening verses of the Koran.

"To clean the house of the devil they burned wild rue, fingered their prayer beads, recited prayers and blew in every corner. Now you'll ask me how the uncle knew. I swear I didn't know this, but romaine is one of the things the Yezidis fear most. Forget touching it or eating it, even mentioning the word is a sin. Yes, really, I was as surprised as you are, I couldn't understand it at all, but when I asked some of the elders they told me it was true. Some say that the Satan they worship is hidden in the romaine, others say that the word *romaine* sounds similar to the word for God in their language. My father could tell you more about it; he knows about these things. Anyway, after this happened my father summoned Hussein and talked to him, gave him advice; after all he'd been his teacher.

"...with my father? Of course you can talk to him, you know he always liked you, but he's asleep now, of course;

it's late. You can come tomorrow. In fact it would be better if you stayed here. Don't go to the hotel at this hour. My wife will get a bed ready for you. Stay for the love of God, we'll have breakfast in the morning, we have so much catching up to do, Ibrahim, we can have *meftune* for lunch, I'm sure you've missed it."

THE ROMAINE FIELD

When we were children we often spent the night at each other's houses. We would take bedding out of the closet and lay it on the floor. The special smell of the furniture in those houses reached out to me from the past. It seemed to me like a message from my former self, shaming me for my disloyalty. As I remembered the creaking wooden stairs, the trembling flames of the gas lamps that were always kept ready because of the frequent electricity cuts, my tender grandmother raising her voice to recite "God hears those who praise him" as I climbed on her back while she was prostrating herself in prayer, the lovely smell that spread through the house from the pots of simmering pink fruit when they were making jam, I felt an uneasy sense of alienation as I asked myself how I could have forgotten all of this...

Mehmet surprised me when he suggested laying out a bed for me, but unlike me he was being genuine. He'd put down roots, while I was swaying in the wind. I was one of those millions of people in the big city whose identities were erased as they strove to be like everyone else.

When I was a child there weren't many hotels or motels here. Mehmet insisted that a "stranger" he hadn't seen in thirty years stay the night, but I didn't stay. I needed to take a walk—my head was spinning from all we'd drunk and everything I'd heard, and my legs felt numb. Of course Mardin wasn't as safe and peaceful as it had been in my childhood, but you never think anything bad is going to happen to you in your own city.

I walked through the deserted streets. Dogs looked up at me from dark corners, but didn't take much of an interest. It would be morning soon. I was curious about the rest of the story, but Mehmet wasn't in a state to continue, probably from emotional weariness, and neither did I have the strength to listen. There was an unnerving silence in the lobby of the hotel that defiled the centuries-old stone madrassa, and there was no one in sight. As soon as I got to my room I flopped onto the bed, but before falling asleep I murmured to myself, "Wow, Hussein, wow."

I passed out immediately afterward, and that night I dreamt of a field where little creatures were swarming out of giant heads of romaine.

GETTING DRUNK ON YOUR OWN BLOOD

"May there be many who kiss your hand, Ibrahim," said Mehmet's father, Uncle Fuat. He continued: "Come, sit here, son, you look as if you could use some myrrh in your coffee, but plain coffee will do the trick. As you can see, I'm well, my boy, old age is hunting me down but I'm in no condition to complain. I was very proud when I heard you were working as a journalist in Istanbul, I saw you on television once, on a news program, do you remember that program? You know, the time they raided a wedding here and killed forty-four people, men, women and children, you were talking about that. There were a lot of rumors going around about that massacre. Some said it was a fight over property, some said it was because of a business deal gone wrong. And they kept asking you about these things, I suppose because you're from Mardin, but the truth of the matter was quite different, son. They all died because of jealousy. The wife of one of the men who was killed, with another man at the wedding... May they repent... These eyes have seen so much blood, son, so much cruelty. That's the way these lands are, there's never any lack of blood, and why is it like this? That's the custom, my son, that's the custom around here. Especially when it comes to honor: no one can think of anything but grabbing a weapon. I'll never forget our late neighbor—he shot his own brother. Our neighbor Hasan was quite a lothario: he was handsome, brave, tall, and lean. His older brother, who was religious, was always angry at him. He threatened him, warned him against sinning and fornicating; he admonished his sister-in-law to tell him if he didn't come home at night. In order to avoid his wrath, the poor woman would put a pair of his shoes outside the door when he didn't come home, so his older brother would think he was there.

"Of course this didn't work, unfortunately. Hasan had a relationship with a woman in a nearby village. She had a pair of twins by him, and he used to go there often. When his older brother found out about this he flew into a rage; he called Hasan to his house and said, 'Make peace with your maker, face any direction you want except the direction of the Kaaba, because I'm going to kill you. Don't you dare face the Kaaba,' he said. (Whatever was going through his mind? Killing your brother isn't a sin, but killing a man facing the Kaaba is?) And he really did shoot him. Yes. Yes, he shot his own brother in the head. Then he went to the village and found that woman. He told her that he was taking the children, that she couldn't take care of them. He said he was going to take them and raise them for now. He was going to find a husband for her, and later he would give the children back. And with that he took the twins back to his own village. He put them in an empty shack and locked it with three padlocks. He told everyone that he would shoot anyone who opened that door—no one was to even go near. The babies cried from hunger and thirst and the heat, but no one dared go open the door. For days the villagers listened to the babies crying, and they themselves were reduced to tears, but there was nothing they could do. I vaguely remember this too; from time to time I think of those babies crying. Their crying grew steadily fainter. The babies were losing strength. It grew fainter and fainter and eventually it stopped. That's what these lands are like, Ibrahim, there's no lack of blood, nor of cruelty. What happened to Hussein is the same kind of thing.

"The man I was just telling you about, when he beat his wife he would take off his clothes and strip her naked. Do you know why? Not because of any perversion or anything that might jump to mind. It was so that no one who heard her screams would come in and intervene. It was so that he could beat her in peace. Men wouldn't come in because the woman was naked, and women wouldn't come in because the man was naked. Do you see this devilish mentality? In spite of this, the woman served her husband flawlessly. She would even peel grapes one by one and offer them to him. What I'm saying is that these are very strange lands.

"Do you know what *harese* is, my son? It's an old Arabic word. The words for determination, greed, and craving are derived from it. I'll tell you what *harese* is, my boy. You know how they call camels the ships of the desert? These blessed animals can walk and walk through the desert without eating or drinking for three weeks, thirsty and hungry; I mean that's how tough they are. But there's a thistle in the desert they're very fond of. Wherever they see this thistle, they bite some off and begin chewing. The sharp thistle lacerates the camel's mouth, and these cuts begin to bleed. The camel likes it even more when the salty taste of the blood mixes with the thistle. So the more it eats the more it bleeds, and the more it bleeds the more it eats. Somehow it can't get its fill of its own blood, and if it's not stopped, the camel will bleed to death. This is called *harese*. As I said earlier, the words for determination, greed, and craving come from it. This is the custom throughout the Middle East, my son. Throughout history people have killed one another without ever realizing that they are actually killing themselves. They become intoxicated by the taste of their own blood.

"What did you say? My hearing isn't as good as it used to be, could you speak a little louder? Yes, yes, this scourge they call ISIS is part of this too. A bloodthirsty organization that emerged from a bloodthirsty land. Anyway, they were the ones who shot Hussein. Don't get excited, I'm going to tell you the whole story, but I have to tell it slowly. There's no hurry. Slow and steady. Some of Mehmet's friends were unlucky, like Raif, like Hussein. Some of them, like you, were able to make something of themselves. It's fate. Everyone in Mardin takes pride in you, we took pride in Hussein as well, but the poor boy became a victim of *barese*. It's a good thing you went to Istanbul and saved yourself. Your parents passed away early, may they rest in God's peace, but you raised yourself and you were very successful.

"Yes, my boy, I know what it is you're curious about. You want to know about the girl who got Hussein into all of this trouble. I mean the Yezidis, the ones who worship Satan.

"Look, son, first of all let's start with the word *Yezidi*. These people are not Yezidi but Ezidi. Their religion is six thousand years old, it's older than Judaism, or Christianity, or Islam. I have some serious books on the subject, but do you read Arabic? That's what I thought; Mehmet can't either. Your generation only knows practical Arabic; Turkish is the language you read and write in. Anyway, I'll tell you.

"The Ezidis face the sun and pray three times a day—some people think this comes from the older forms of sun worship. It's such an old religion that no one can remember its origins. You know we have a lot of Assyrian monasteries here: well, underneath the Deyrulzafaran monastery there's a sun temple—it was built four thousand years ago. They also go and pray there. According to their beliefs, there is God and seven angels. The chief angel is the Peacock Angel, the Tawuse Melek. Yes, the chief angel is an angel in the form of a peacock.

"When God created humanity and asked the angel to bow before them he refused. 'I was created from fire,' he said, 'they were created from earth.' He was banished from heaven because he said 'I will not bow before them, they should bow down before me.' And this is where the part about Satan comes in. Because Satan was banished from heaven in the later religions, they thought that the Peacock Angel was Satan. And they announced that these people worshipped Satan. However, the Peacock Angel repented after being banished from heaven. He wept for seven thousand years, and his tears extinguished all the fires and filled the seas. After that, God, or rather Ezd, forgave him and took him back and made him the chief angel. This is what the Ezidi believe, my son. They consider the Peacock Angel sacred, and they never mention Satan. If you ask whether the Peacock Angel is good or evil, they'll tell you that he's both good and evil, that is he's the angel of both evil and good. They're good people, but they've been persecuted throughout history because it was thought that they worshipped Satan. Somehow their situation never improved, and their population began to dwindle. They refer to themselves that way too, they call themselves 'the tree of humanity's broken branch.'

"When ISIS came, another massacre began. ISIS raided their villages and killed the men: they cut off their heads and then burned them, they made the girls and young women concubines, they raped them, they started teaching the children to hate Ezidis. There was a lot of cruelty, son, a lot. Those who could escape fled to Shingal, their sacred mountain, and from there they crossed the border into Turkey. They were kept in separate camps. A wretched, miserable people; if you saw what they've been through it would tear you apart.

"Let's get to what you're most curious about, that is, Hussein and the girl called Meleknaz. I summoned Hussein here, I talked to him, counseled him. I told him that he was not going to be able to marry this Ezidi girl—it's forbidden by Muslims and the other religions and indeed even by the Ezidi themselves. But he said they're good people, Uncle Fuat, they're pure-hearted; and if you could see Meleknaz...

"'I know, my son,' I said, 'and I also know that this business about worshipping Satan is nonsense. They're good people, but this is what tradition dictates. I'm trying to protect you from Mardin, you and that poor girl, and the blind baby too. You know that there are a lot of ISIS supporters here, and they wouldn't let you or the girl live. Now you'll say that they abduct Ezidi girls, but there's a difference. They were following thousands of years of tradition when they were enslaving those girls. They used them as concubines, they sold them in slave markets, and sometimes they bought ten-year-old girls for a pack of cigarettes. But you want to marry her, and there is no chance that they would accept this. A Muslim and an Ezidi can't marry, can't be man and wife. I know it's nonsense, complete nonsense. You know that I'm an open-minded person, but you know that in these lands belief comes before everything else, even if it's superstition, or simply wrong. This road leads to death, Hussein, I'm your teacher.'

"I told him to let go of this love. I did what I could but I couldn't convince him—the only thing he said was that he was going to rescue that girl, he didn't say anything else. He was madly in love, and I started feeling curious about the girl. Who was this girl who caused Hussein, who was a devout Muslim, to embark on this madness? What kind of blind passion was it that caused Hussein to turn against his fiancée, his mother, his sister, his teacher, and indeed all of Mardin? Where is this girl now, Hussein, I asked him, and he said she's missing, uncle, I'm trying to find her. She left her baby and fled. Then he told me the story.

"Romaine lettuce is a great sin for the Ezidi, one of their greatest sins. There are a lot of different stories about this, perhaps even they themselves don't know, but that's the way it's been for thousands of years. I saw that Hussein was growing impatient—he could barely sit still—that he wanted to go look for that girl as soon as possible. He was squirming because he didn't want to be disrespectful to his teacher. You remember, don't you, what a well-behaved boy he always was. In the end he couldn't stand it, and when he asked me to excuse him I realized nothing I'd told him was going to make any difference. The poor boy kissed my hand and rushed out of here as fast as he could, toward the angel of death that was awaiting him.

THE SACRED MESOPOTAMIAN SUN

"Aysel, maybe I'm overwhelming you with my questions, but please answer. What did Hussein do when the girl ran away?"

"What do you expect, he started searching for her like a madman, he turned the entire city upside down."

"And then?"

"Everyone in the city was talking about it. A group of ISIS supporters stopped Hussein in the street; they said they knew he was looking for that she-devil, and that they were looking for her themselves. When they found her they would kill her on the spot. If he found her and insisted on marrying her, they would shoot both of them."

"I imagine Hussein wasn't put off by these threats."

"No, of course not. And because he's smart, he found the girl before they did."

"Where did she go? To the refugee camp?"

"No, that camp is too far away. She wouldn't have even attempted to make that trip. Besides, she didn't have any money: that's why Hussein didn't even look for her at the camps."

"So where did he look for her, then?"

"He guessed she was hiding someplace that was sacred for the Yezidis."

"Meaning?"

"The sun temple."

"The temple beneath the Deyrulzafaran monastery?"

"Yes, exactly. I suppose she thought that the sun or Satan or whatever would protect her there."

Two hours later I was catching my breath in the Deyrulzafaran monastery, five kilometers outside Mardin.

A little earlier I'd received permission to enter from the Assyrian chief priest, Father Gabriel, whose eyes reflected a tenderness that made it clear he would never harm any living creature. They were polite enough to allow me to spend some time alone in this strange, cave-like place, or rather when I asked them for this they agreed. The sun temple was constructed from giant blocks of stone that were leaned against each other. There was no mortar or anything—the tons of rock above my head were held in place by a keystone that had been forced into place, and it had been standing for almost four thousand years. When I thought about this I shuddered. One day it was bound to collapse, perhaps in an earthquake. I looked around for traces of Meleknaz in that cold, crypt-like temple. I wondered how she'd come here, why she'd come here, which stone she'd crouched beside—was it here? Did she cry, did she miss her baby, or did her fear of sin block out everything else? I hadn't known anything about these Ezidi everyone had been talking to me about recently; in fact I'd called them Yezidi. I'd heard that they worshipped Satan, but that didn't really mean anything to me.

Years ago, after a long and difficult process reminiscent of a snake shedding its skin, I'd cut all my ties to God and Satan. And at university I'd seen a play called *Mahmud and Yezida* about a Muslim boy and an Ezidi girl. I remember being amazed when a circle was drawn around the Ezidis and they were unable to move out of it. I thought this was some kind of fantasy, but my friends told me it was true. I wondered if the ISIS militants were going to draw a circle around Meleknaz when they found her. Would they lock her in the prison in her own mind?

The only thing that kept the stone sun temple from being in complete darkness was a small rectangular opening through which the Mesopotamian sun seeped. A vision formed in my mind of the first light of morning illuminating the face of a young woman who was praying. It was as if I actually saw the girl. The mystical atmosphere was making me dizzy. I'd lost my sense of time and place in this gloomy crypt—I had the feeling that whatever I had once been, I had been transformed into a very different kind of creature. Becoming aware of the great difference between the age of the world and my own age had a stupefying effect akin to sunstroke.

If Ibrahim, an atheist journalist who had entered the digital age, just come from a complicated twenty-first-century metropolis, was feeling this, it made me dizzy to think about the effect it might have on someone in ancient times who lived in an imaginary world of tales and legends. I was very curious about Meleknaz; I suppose I was thinking about her even more than I was about Hussein. What kind of girl was she, what did she look like, was she rebellious, was she wild, was she pathetic, was she clever, or perhaps she was all of these things at the same time? I couldn't picture her because there was no photograph of her in the album Aysel had given me, but in a very strange way it was as if I could feel her soul in that dark temple.

It was as if I was having some kind of experience there: I felt cut off from the material world, even though I didn't believe in any of these things. My professor at journalism school used to say they were empty beliefs. He said these empty beliefs were truly empty. They didn't reflect the truth, but that at the same time, all of humanity's creativity and art was indebted to these beliefs. "Do you know," he asked, "why the Mayan ziggurats have steps on all four sides? The Mayans were terrified of the snakes in the jungle, so they made them sacred. They arranged the pyramids so that no shade would fall on the snakes regardless of the time of day or the position of the sun. What was the result? A nonsensical belief gave birth to a magnificent esthetic. Like all of the world's temples, altars, and pyramids. So some things shouldn't be dismissed as empty beliefs—without them, human culture would not have come into being, and neither would architecture or music or literature. At first Darwin went to the Galápagos Islands to prove the existence of God, and Faraday was also trying to do this."

These words came to my mind as I sat in the sun temple with my back against a stone, and I can't lie, I was looking for Meleknaz. I was looking for some trace of her. The strange thing is that I did find something, but by touch rather than sight. First my hand brushed against something soft in the darkness, and when I held it up to look at it in the supposedly sacred light trapped in that chasm, I saw that it was a handkerchief: thin, white, soft, a handkerchief like any other handkerchief. The only difference was that there was a red peacock embroidered on the corner, a black-and-red Peacock Angel. I thought I detected the scent of a woman on this handkerchief, but perhaps I was imagining it. I now had something that had belonged to Meleknaz, a handkerchief with which she'd dried her tears. For the first time in my life I was touching a carefully embroidered Peacock Angel. The angel of evil and good, the greatest queen of regret and repentance, an extraordinary combination of Satan and Angel that moves beyond good and evil. Meleknaz and the Peacock Angel, who filled the oceans with tears, were slowly coming together. In the distance a woman was crying out: "The tree of humanity's broken branch."

I was on the verge of tears. Pull yourself together, Ibrahim, I said, pull yourself together, don't get carried away by nonsense; don't get swept up in this city's broken down fairy-tale atmosphere.

FATHER GABRIEL RECOUNTS

"Ibrahim, we're very pleased by your visit. Of course we read your articles, we're proud that someone from Mardin became such a national success. Yes, what you say is true, when this building was built they mixed local saffron into the mortar, that's why the monastery is a saffron yellow.

"Yes, your question is reasonable, I understand your journalistic curiosity; it's normal to ask why an Assyrian monastery was built on top of a pagan temple. But I'm not the one to ask, you'd have to ask the people who built the monastery. A lot of time has passed, and the sun temple has lost its significance. I suspect that was the reason. In any event, our building is new, very new. The monastery is only sixteen hundred years old, and the temple below is four thousand years old. Don't laugh, I'm being serious, in this region sixteen hundred years ago is like yesterday. Did you notice the inscription above the door? They're Solomon's psalms, in Aramaic, that is, in our language. Our spiritual ancestors built this monastery, may Allah's blessings be upon them. Yes, yes, we say Allah when we're speaking Turkish. In Aramaic we say Eli. Anyway, aren't Eli, Eloi, Ilah, and Allah the same thing? The different names of a single creator. The last words that Jesus Christ uttered on the cross? Yes, he spoke in Aramaic, of course. So you know the history of Christianity. *Eli, Eli, lama sabachthani.* God, why hast thou forsaken me? We speak the same language today in the monastery, the language of the Bible. What difference does it make once you have belief in your heart, we're all his creatures, aren't we?

"Well now you've asked me a difficult question. The Yezidi don't use any of these hallowed names for the creator. And I don't think they believe in him. There's the Peacock Angel. May Allah rescue them from their error, because they're living in sin. Yes, yes, just as with Islam we see them as deviant; the Jews see them that way too. But no matter how hard you try, they won't give up on that blind belief. Who would worship a peacock, Ibrahim, you're a sound Muslim, tell me for the love of Allah, what kind of belief is that? No matter what religion you're from, you can't mention Satan in their presence. I pray that the Great Creator puts them on the right path, but they're very obstinate. They're the most persecuted people in history, but they refuse to change. Their faith is extremely strict.

"So you're curious about that Yezidi girl, that poor girl Meleknaz. I don't understand why you're curious, but I'll tell you about her. One of the priests heard the sound of crying from the temple, and when he went to look he saw a girl sitting on the floor, crying. He brought her here. We tried Turkish and Aramaic, but she only understood Arabic and Kurdish. We asked her name and she said Meleknaz. Whatever their religion, we never turn anyone away from this monastery, Ibrahim. We put her in a room so she could rest a bit, we gave her some food and some clothes. She slept for a long time, until the late Hussein came here in a rush. He told us everything, that the girl was Yezidi but that he was engaged to her. Of course it's not our place to warn him, but we did say that this was forbidden in both Islam and Christianity, but he didn't listen to us. He took Meleknaz and left. We never saw either of them again. Of course we heard about him being shot and his stay in the hospital, and his tragic end in Germany. May he rest in peace, he was such a good and honest man, he left this world at a young age because of that girl and her deviant belief. Believe me, we were deeply saddened.

"I didn't know he was your childhood friend, so you came here because of him. Please give his grieving family our condolences. May Allah grant them patience.

"...The girl, Meleknaz...yes, she was a skinny, dark girl, her face was so thin that her eyes looked large, her eyes had an amazing sparkle, sometimes angry, sometimes full of hate, sometimes defiant. How can I put it? It was as if she had a secret she wasn't going to reveal, it made you curious. Perhaps if she spoke she would be less enigmatic, but somehow her silence made her seem deeper. In short, we couldn't figure the girl out, but it was clear that there was a powerful soul in that thin body. We remembered her for a long time.

"No, I don't have the slightest idea where she is now. You want to see the sun temple, of course, after talking about it so much you have to see it. I hope you get a good article out of this."

THE FORMER FIANCÉE

The following day, Aysel, wearing a black headscarf, took me to the mansion of Hussein's former fiancée, Safiye. She'd finally given in to my constant pleading: I was so consumed by curiosity that I risked being disrespectful to a grieving family. Like the other houses here, it was built from soft Mardin stone, with elaborate carvings on its facade. When the stone is exposed to air it oxidizes; it turns red and takes on an enchanting air. It was a large family mansion that had been home to who knows how many generations.

Safiye received us in the living room on the lower floor. Even though she was a bit plump, as soon as I saw her I thought "My God, how beautiful she is." In the Middle East, where beauty is only sought in eyes that are as deep and dark as the desert night, plump women are considered more desirable, and her slight double chin added to her appeal. At first Safiye had the air of a sad and heartbroken princess, but after Aysel introduced me I could see the volcanic anger that was seething within her. It seemed almost as if her sense of having been dishonored was stronger than the pain of having lost someone she loved. Flaring her beautiful and shapely nostrils, she said, "That man, your brother..." She couldn't even bring herself to utter Hussein's name. "Forgive me, Aysel, but that brother of yours was an ungrateful and thankless man, he was sick, yes, yes, he was a truly sick man. What kind of person would destroy his life for a Satan worshipper dressed in rags, for that sniveling girl. He had everything going for him; on top of that she had a baby, on top of that the baby was blind, and on top of that he wasn't even the baby's father. I don't know what sin I committed for that brother of yours to be so remorseless to me. My father hangs his head in shame, my mother cries all the time, our relatives are avoiding us, and at my young age I've been marked as a rejected fiancée. You know I like you, Aysel, I like you a lot, but I can't help it, I hope that Allah makes that brother of yours pay for what he did." For a moment I was taken aback by the way she was speaking as if Hussein were still alive. "I hope he pays such a price that he understands what it means to toy with someone's honor."

Then she uttered a string of curses. A richer collection of curses I'd never heard—they struck me with terror. I even wanted to take notes. My favorite one, the one that really stuck in my mind, was "May Allah give him scabies but no fingernails to scratch with." What did that even mean? What a terrible torture.

Safiye was speaking of her former fiancé as if he were still alive, as if Hussein hadn't lost his life abroad, as if his remains hadn't been brought back and buried in the village cemetery. It seemed that there were sorrows that could overshadow even death, that there were actions that couldn't be forgiven even in death. At that moment Aysel said what had been going through my mind. "Safiye, dear," she said, "I understand your pain, but we're in pain too. My brother Hussein is dead now, don't speak ill of the dead, we're wounded as well."

At this, glittering tears began to pour from her eyes and stream down Safiye's cheeks. "I loved him so much, I loved him so much, I was head over heels in love with him. Somehow I just can't accept that he's dead, that he's gone, now I ask myself if Hussein is gone, is he gone forever now, he was here but he's gone, how could something like that happen? I get very confused, and at the same time I can't forgive him for what he did to me."

This girl's mind was like a ball of yarn in which anger and love, pride and humiliation, mourning and the desire for revenge were inextricably intertwined. I felt a bit sorry for her.

"I wonder," she said, "If there's any connection between his death and the curses I showered on him. I cursed him from the bottom of my heart, I sent him curses, I prostrated myself in prayer and beseeched Allah to make him suffer for what he did to me. I wonder if I was the one who killed him, I can't get that out of my head."

POETRY

As I was parting from Aysel that evening, she told me at the last moment to wait; she'd forgotten something. Then she pressed a sheaf of papers into my hand. I asked her what it was, and she said she thought they were the love poems Hussein had written to that girl. "I glance at them from time to time. I have no intention of reading through them, but... I think they're love poems; the girl left them in her room. My mother said to burn them—perhaps they're magic spells, perhaps they are, who knows, that band of demons is capable of anything. I was just about to burn them when it occurred to me that they might be of use to you. Read them if you want or just throw them away, but be careful—don't you get bewitched as well."

As she gave me the letters and warned me not to get bewitched she gave me an affectionate little smile. It pleased me to realize she felt close to me; I'd always been very fond of that almond-eyed girl. I watched her walk away over paving stones that had been polished over thousands of years. She had a black mourning scarf covering her head; she was wearing a blue sweater, and on her shoulders, in the words of the poet, there was anguish, endless anguish.

When I got back to the hotel I sipped a strong coffee as I looked over the papers. This had to be Hussein's handwriting: it was a tidy and light, in the *Ruq'ah* style. But I could no longer read Arabic (though I could still speak it), and there was no chance I could understand this. I could only vaguely make out a few things here and there, and occasionally I misunderstood the words. The *Ruq'ah* was even more difficult for me to read. Anyway, I was in Mardin, and there were a lot of people here who knew Arabic: just about everyone. In Istanbul I would have had to go to a university or a translation bureau to find someone who knew Arabic.

To cut to the chase, it was Uncle Fuat who neatly transcribed the poems into the Latin alphabet and made it possible for me to understand them. He was fond of poetry: he translated them eagerly and gave them to me the next day. The language was poetic. However much it's possible to translate poetry.

And what poems my childhood friend had written!

It was filled with the spicy words of thousands of years of Arabic and Persian poetry, from pre-Islamic times and well as from later periods. Love, passion, longing, desert, the love-crazed, nectar, moonlight; it made me feel as if I were wandering in an Oriental garden with a thousand-and-one flowers and fragrances:

Don't dare to think I complain, like a grape crushed
beneath the feet of love
I am transformed into ruby-colored wine
This is why I'm willing to be crushed.

Another poem went like this:

I am the one who was drunk before grapevines were created
I was the one who was dissipated by love for you before
you were born.

In the poems there was frequent mention of Jamshid, Goliath, Rustam, Afrasiab, and Semiramis:

If Goliath were to come between us, my angelic one
I would become David with my slingshot of love.

And later he wrote,

I was as madly enamored as Solomon was when he was
smitten by the Queen of Sheba's ankles.

Was it possible for anyone not to be moved by this? As if these weren't written to a wretched girl who'd escaped ISIS and was living in a refugee camp but love psalms to the Queen of Sheba. I wanted to know what Hussein's burning love, his heartsick passion, was like. Were loves like this particular to the East, was this some kind of *harese* by means of which people ruined themselves? Can the phrase "in the name of love" be translated into any other language? Coming as I did from the passionless world of faceless city people who are governed by expediency, I envied Hussein's deep passion. What kind of passion was it that drove him to write these verses and dragged him to the valley of death, like Majnun in the burning desert? What could Meleknaz have thought when she read these poems? She was in the presence of a pleading love. *You have the strength of Rustem*, he called to her,

> *As for me, I'm a miserable wretch*
> *You're the one who's strong*
> *I'm the one who's weak*
> *Because I've been wounded by the arrow of love.*

Was there any chance that this unfortunate girl living in that squalid tent was seized by feminine pride when she read these verses? The victim was transformed into a goddess. Each of the names Hussein used had the vastness of Mesopotamia behind it; every image contained a historical reference that was common to both their heritages. He spoke of the wind that the Prophet's horse Burak drank—if it were me I would have spoken of Rocinante—while he named his eternal love Zuleyla—I would have said Dulcinea—while he spoke of cities such as Balkh, Bukhara, and Samarkand—I would have said Istanbul, Paris, Rome, and London—I have to confess that I was seized by a deep shame because I felt like a tourist in my own country.

For years I had lived in this country as if I were a foreigner. That's how I was educated. I used to identify with the cowboys in the movies we watched as children at the Lale Cinema in Mardin, but on my first visit to Europe it struck me forcefully that I was not a cowboy but an Indian—I wasn't white, I was black. A novel I read some years ago, I think the title was *Bliss*, spoke of how the literate people of this country were like trapeze artists falling into the void. We had let go of the trapeze of the East, but failed to grasp the trapeze of the West.

ANOTHER ANGEL COMES FROM THE FAR END OF THE WORLD

I kept my phone off the whole time I was in Mardin, so that there would be no ringing or message tones at the wrong place and time. I made a decision to look at my phone every evening to see who had called, but I was so drawn in by the fairy-tale atmosphere, and when I got back to the hotel in the evening I was so drowsy with wine, that I neglected to do this. In the world of Istanbul journalism, automatic replies such as "out of range" or "currently unavailable" were considered a grave sin. Even though I know that "out of sight is out of mind," I preferred to get caught up in the sleepiness of Mesopotamia. That was until one night when my phone, which was on vibrate, began shaking on the table until it seemed ready to jump off. It's impossible not to answer a phone that rings in the middle of the night, and that was especially true when I saw the chief editor's name on the screen.

The moment I answered the phone in a raspy, tired, and groggy manner, the chief editor lit into me. Where the hell was I, they'd been trying to reach me for days, wasn't I checking my messages, the general manager kept asking about me, they were jumping through hoops, and so forth and so on.

I was now wide awake, and as I listened I tried to frame my answer in my mind. In the end, when the editor had to pause for breath, I took the opportunity to interject. I apologized and said I was working on something interesting. It had to do with Syrian refugees, Ezidi camps, ISIS massacres and rapes. I had a story that was going to attract a lot of interest, and indeed I wanted to do a series of articles. Of course, that was if the newspaper's management "found it suitable." If they didn't, I would like to use some of my vacation time and stay here for a while.

"Vacation time!" he said, "You're exactly where you need to be. Tomorrow journalists are going to be flocking there. We're sending a photographer out to join you."

I suddenly wondered what was going on. Had Hussein's story suddenly attracted a lot of attention?

"Don't you have any idea of what's going on in the world? Angelina Jolie is going there tomorrow. She's going to visit the camps as the United Nations Goodwill Ambassador. Reporters are coming from all over the world, do you understand?"

"Of course," I stuttered. "So Angelina Jolie is coming here! What an incredible opportunity."

"Look," said the editor, "I don't know what you're doing there, but fortune has smiled on you. Take care of all of the accreditations right away, we want some good pictures of Jolie with the refugees. You and Hakan do whatever you have to do. Oh, and there's one more thing: it wouldn't kill you to drink nothing but water for a few days, would it? Just a few days."

Then he ended the call abruptly; it was clear they were very angry. A journalist who can't be reached is either dead or willing to risk being fired.

I looked at my screen, and it was a mess! So many missed calls. Eight calls from my ex-wife, many more from the newspaper, a few friends and so forth. WhatsApp. Viber, text messages. A young woman I'd been seeing who wrote *Where R U* followed by a string of emojis: surprised yellow faces, sad yellow faces, smiling yellow faces, angry red faces, hearts pulsing as if they were pumping blood... All of this now seemed to me like signals coming from outer space. What did any of these symbols have to do with the four-thousand-year-old sun temple? Perhaps they had a deep relevance that I didn't understand, but I couldn't grasp it. I wondered if there was a peacock emoji. I looked, and I found something, but I couldn't decide if that little image was a peacock or a turkey. I imagine it would be a great sin to mistake a turkey for a peacock; after all one was an animal and the other was an angel. I put Meleknaz's handkerchief next to my pillow, turned my phone's sound on and abandoned myself to the angel of sleep. My last thought before falling asleep was to get Mehmet to help me get permission from the governor.

The woman really is beautiful. Her uncommonly clear skin, her enormous eyes and her high cheekbones seemed to say "I'm different, I'm different from everyone else." She walked through the crowd of reporters toward the tents. She'd covered her head with a black shawl, and her expression was serious, not sorrowful but serious.

Syrian refugees were reaching out to touch her, and she touched all of them, like the touch of an angel. She raised her hand to stop the security personnel who didn't want the wretched refugees to get too close to her. She patted the children's heads and smiled.

Suddenly we came face-to-face. Angelina Jolie's moist, bright eyes were looking at me. All of us were enchanted.

I handed her a handkerchief, a handkerchief with a Peacock Angel embroidered in the corner in black-and-red thread. She took it and gave me a questioning look. I told her that the handkerchief belonged to an Ezidi woman, that perhaps she'd embroidered the Peacock Angel herself. This was the Ezidis' angel, it was not Satan, as everyone believed. Please listen to me, believe me, these people are not children of Satan, they're the children of the sun, the children of the three mountains, the children of the *kalam*. Their holy book, Mushafi Resh, that is, the Black Book, is lost; it's passed orally from generation to generation.

These words are sacred to them. That's why they're called the children of the *kalam*, that is, the children of the word. They've been persecuted, they're on the point of being wiped out. The woman who embroidered this handkerchief has a blind baby. We know that you're very compassionate, the whole world knows, you've adopted dozens of babies. I think you should adopt this blind baby as well, restore her sight. We'll find her missing mother, I've been looking for her. Her name means "angel," just like yours. How strange, another angel has come to rescue the children of the Peacock Angel.

Then something happened that I didn't understand. Angelina Jolie's face turned into the Peacock Angel. "I'm already her mother," she said, "I gave birth to that baby. Are you an idiot? She was born blind in both eyes so she wouldn't see the evil that's being done to the Ezidis in this world, so she won't see the cruelty, the babies dying of thirst in the mountains, the women who were abducted by ISIS and sold in slave markets, little girls with lacerated wombs after being raped by ten militants in the belief that being raped ten times will turn her into a Muslim; so she won't witness the savage extermination of the race of people I brought down from God's world to this one. Do you think that you understand everything that happens in this world? Your heart is closed to the angels. Get out of here, you miserable human!"

JOLIE THE ANGEL

The following day was quite different from my dream. The private jet that brought Angelina Jolie landed at the remote Mardin airport at 20:00. The deputy governor and an official delegation received her and the UN representatives who were with her. The journalists were kept at a distance, and everyone was climbing over each other to get a picture from behind a row of policemen.

The delegation whisked Angelina into an official black car that immediately sped away. We didn't know at the time, but we found out later that she was taken to the Hilton Garden Inn, which is outside Mardin and on the road to the ruins of Dara. When Hakan the photographer and I found out we went to the hotel, but all we could see was the fountain at the entrance. The hotel had been cordoned off, and the roads were blocked. It wasn't just us; they weren't letting anyone in. The bazooka-like lenses hanging from Hakan's neck didn't help us at all, and our efforts to get a photo from a distance were to no avail.

"Man," I said to Hakan, "what the hell are we doing here? They're not going to let us see the woman. It's as if she's some kind of sacred treasure, but she's just a person like us. Man, she's not an angel, she's not a goddess, why is everyone going so crazy? The woman is probably going into the bathroom now, she's going to take a shower, she'll put on her bathrobe and have something to eat in her room, then she'll get a good sleep while we stand out here, miserably shoving each other and craning our necks."

"But the newspaper is going to want at least one picture," objected Hakan. "What are we going to do?"

"Maybe one of the other photographers got a picture. Ask around and see if anyone got one. If that doesn't work we can download a picture from the internet and edit it—the woman is constantly going to camps in Afghanistan and Pakistan."

I became irritated by the crowds and the commotion, I kept complaining about this woman who wasn't aware of any of this. She'd woken me from a dream and brought me back to the modern world and to journalism. And I wanted to stay within the atmosphere of the angel. I wasn't interested in this angel, but in the other angel, the one who had gone missing. And I suppose I really was angry at Jolie; her coming here from the glittering world of Hollywood and visiting the camps for two hours wasn't going to do anything but add to the pain of the people there. If I got the chance to talk to her, I'd say that these people are all here because of your policies, or rather your government's policies. What right did you have to send your planes and soldiers and ships across the ocean and destroy these people's country, to bring more bloodshed to the already bloodstained lands of the Middle East, fooling the world with lies about weapons of mass destruction, making millions of people homeless, spreading terror in our lands! Was this what the United Nations was established for?

Of course the poor woman wasn't responsible for any of this, she didn't dictate these policies, but she didn't realize that she was just going to increase the suffering of the people whose pain she was coming to lighten. She was highlighting the chasm between her world and that of these cold, hopeless, ragged refugees. She was a symbol that reminded them another life was possible, increasing their despair, deepening their pain. Because after she got on her private jet and returned to her glittering life, they would continue to bury children who'd died from carbon monoxide poisoning from the stoves in those tents.

Two years ago I interviewed a student who'd been tortured by the police. They had locked him in a cellar and tortured him until he was crippled. For some reason he became obsessed with a canary in a cage that was hanging in the cellar. He told me he had hated that canary. Its beautiful song had reminded him of the outside world, of springtime, lovers strolling arm in arm—it made him think of freedom, and this made everything even more painful. The canary became a symbol of beauty, and he hated it because there was no place for beauty in that cellar. Now I was thinking that perhaps Jolie was a canary: an angel disguised not as a peacock but as a canary.

We went back to the hotel and went over the day's news. Thanks to a touching example of solidarity among news photographers, Hakan had managed to get a picture from another photographer of Jolie leaving the plane. We'd managed to save the day.

In the evening Mehmet once again demonstrated his hospitality by inviting me to dinner (his wife made lamb shoulder with red plums, something I hadn't had since childhood). Thankfully he'd come through for me. And though he hadn't been able to reach the governor at that hour, he had called his personal assistant and learned that the following day Angelina Jolie and her entourage would be going to a refugee camp in Midyat. We were going to be there before her, of course.

THE THRILL OF DIVORCE

The next morning I was woken by a call from my ex-wife, Aslı. Even before my alarm had gone off I was confronted by her irritable voice shouting at me and asking where I'd been. It's annoying to have a woman shouting at you that early in the morning. I don't know what kind of woman you're picturing, but I'm not going to conceal the fact that my wife, or rather my ex-wife, is beautiful. Like so many others in our twenty-first-century cities, she had long legs and stylish sandy hair. She was an attractive woman who dressed elegantly, and like all beautiful women she was frightening, and she was unsettling, all because she'd grown up hearing how beautiful she was. Even when she was still at school she'd learned to wrap the adolescent boys who were so taken by her around her little finger. She organized her life like a commander who grasped that her beauty and her sexuality were important weapons. She had an attitude of superiority to men that hadn't occurred in our mothers' time. She never fell for anyone; she would wait for men to fall in love with her. She would never serve, but rather expected to be served. She expected men to open doors for her, she expected to be courted, to be bought expensive gifts, to be praised. On social occasions she would tell a story she and her husband both knew, and she would expect her husband to keep quiet.

It's as if such women are waiting in ambush to take revenge in a single lifetime for the hundreds of years of oppression women have suffered in this Islamic country. I can make this generalization comfortably, because every time I became involved with a beautiful woman it ended in disillusionment. I've become accustomed to seeing angel-faced women as devils, and that's why whenever I see a beautiful woman I think bad things. These are the high-heeled women in the skyscrapers, plazas, modern workplaces, shopping malls where they sell luxury goods, and the restaurants with foreign names. Women who drink regularly, who mix English words, pronounced with an American accent, into almost every sentence, who are well-educated, who exude sweet fragrance. Women who don't care the least about their virginity or who they have their first experience with. (When a lover like that was leaving me and I said something about how she wouldn't forget her first man, she laughed at me and asked if I was living in the Middle Ages. Though I was simply trying to comfort myself with the Chinese saying that "women remember their first love and men remember their last." Contrary to what people think, men now have more need to rest their heads on the velvet pillow of romanticism.)

"You never answer your phone, you don't return my calls, you're always so irresponsible. As if I don't have enough to do without having to chase you down. Be a little civilized." She was shouting at me, telling me to be civilized. I didn't say anything, I just listened. I just let her get it out of her system, so she could calm down. Because I knew that when she was so completely worked up like this she wouldn't hear anything I said—indeed, anything I said would serve no purpose other than to irritate her even more.

As she carried on, I had a pleasant memory. We experienced our most beautiful, most passionate lovemaking after our divorce. We were married less than a year, but we both wanted to be free. Married life had become a suffocating nightmare for both of us. At divorce court, both of our lawyers cited irreconcilable differences and stated that both parties had agreed to separation. So one afternoon in May, after giving us some fatherly advice, the judge granted our divorce. We'd entered the courthouse as husband and wife, and we left as two single people, two divorced people. It was a warm spring day. I felt a sense of lightness, I felt cheerful, and I could see that Aslı felt the same way. I invited her to a farewell meal. We went to a small, pleasant Italian restaurant. We drank red wine and had a Mediterranean-style lunch, and we laughed a lot—we rose like two hot-air balloons that had cast off their sandbags.

I don't know what happened afterward. We left the restaurant, I took her home, to the house I'd bought and furnished and would never see again—I left it to her—and we jumped urgently into bed. We made love with a passion and desire we'd never experienced before; we reached the highest notes of pleasure, we flew, we rose above the mountains and then flung ourselves into the void. We dove into the depths of the sea, we passed under the rainbow.

"You're not even returning your lawyer's calls," Aslı was shouting, "You're mindboggling, you are!"

This was an expression in the new Istanbul slang, a slang that I felt sounded ignorant. Why such beautiful women debase themselves—themselves and their fellow women—I'll never understand. I decided that the time had come. I said, "My love..." but I shouldn't have. She immediately lit into me again.

"I'm not your love, you'd better get that into your head, you idiot, the only thing I want from you is for you to sign the house over to me like you promised. Is that so difficult, what kind of person are you!"

It has always amazed me how two people who become intertwined with each other as they make love, who become as intimate as it's possible to be, can later become so alienated from each other, and indeed even try to hurt each other. How strange: such tremendous delight at first, and so much pain later.

"Fine," I said. "Sorry, I was sent to Mardin, I'm working on some important news, I'll sign the papers as soon as I get back." She was silent for a moment, then she asked in a suspicious tone if I promised, and I said I promised. Do you swear, she asked, and I said I swore on her life. (I think I just wanted to tease her.) Don't clown around, she said. I'm not, I said, I swear on the last time we made love, it will be the first thing I do when I get back.

"I've forgotten about that already," she said. "You go on fantasizing if you want." I was careless enough to ask why she was in such a big hurry, was she getting married again or something? She laid into me for this. What business was it of mine? Who was I to interfere in her life: the people in her life were none of my business, and so forth and so on.

I hung up the phone calmly. I wasn't angry at her, but it was clear she was still very angry at me. When I was in Istanbul I was angry at her too. But here in Mardin, in this hushed, indifferent world that flows slowly like water, caught up in Hussein's fate, Meleknaz, and the drama of three million refugees, that anger had vanished.

My life in Istanbul seemed so distant to me now. It looked as small as if I were looking at it through the wrong end of a telescope. Time flowed backward in Mardin, the place was seeping into every particle of me. I was curious about Meleknaz, I wanted to find out where she was. I'd never even seen a picture of her, this girl who was a mixture of devil and angel. I wanted to look into those eyes that no one had been able to describe. She must have had a strange appearance—or personality—because everyone who saw her was struck so forcefully. According to Mehmet, when Hussein was bringing her home from the camp he pleaded with her not to tell anyone she was Ezidi. He begged her, he said his people had mistaken ideas about the Ezidi, that if they found out it would be a disaster—"For my sake, tell them you're Muslim." At this point in the conversation I asked Mehmet what language they spoke. In fact the girl knew a little Turkish, although her native languages were Arabic and Kurdish. So they had no problem communicating, because Hussein knew Arabic. In Mardin everyone used to speak Arabic at home, and even though my Arabic is a bit rusty now, we all used to speak it fluently.

Hussein's pleading was of no use. She dug her heels in, saying she would not deny her religion, and furthermore, among the Ezidi, lying was considered the greatest sin. She said he could cut her and make her bleed, but she still wouldn't lie. So they decided that she just wouldn't say anything about religion; it wouldn't even occur to anyone to ask a Syrian girl named Meleknaz if she was Muslim. This way Meleknaz wouldn't have to lie, and no one in the family would know the truth. But that romaine—Hussein kept going on about it—how could he have ever guessed that a green leaf would turn his life upside down?

The girl kept quiet as she'd promised. She didn't say anything, she kept quiet, until the romaine disaster. Aunt Adviye and Aysel had been growing accustomed to this strange, unsettling, silent girl. She never spoke, but sometimes she sang lullabies to her child in an unknown language; she was harmless, she ate next to nothing. She and her blind baby stayed in one of the rooms on the top floor that looked onto the back courtyard; there was no question of anyone living together in sin under that roof. Aunt Adviye would believe that the sun rose in the west or that the Euphrates was flowing backward before she would believe that Hussein would do anything "immoral."

THE CHILDREN

OF *KALAM*

For us journalists, Angelina Jolie's visit to the camps the next day was just like the previous day, a complete disappointment. We couldn't get past the security perimeter and reach Jolie, and again we only saw the woman from a distance, although Hakan was able to get a few good shots with his bazooka-like lenses. We were thankful we at least had that. In any event, I was much more interested in the refugees than I was in Jolie.

From my point of view, Jolie's only significance was the odd coincidence that her name meant "angel." I consider myself a sane man, but occasionally I find it difficult to resist the attraction of finding a metaphysical side to coincidences like this. I think all people have something like this. I think that even if we don't admit it, we all like to think that our existence, our lives, are not bound to some meaningless, nonsensical coincidences but have a deeper meaning that we can't grasp. For me, having several different angels lined up in front of me became something like a pleasant game. But my thoughts and my curiosity were slowly shifting from my childhood friend Hussein toward Meleknaz. As for Angelina Jolie, human beings can't live without mythology. Modern people in a technological age without mythology created a new mythology, and she was a new Olympian goddess whose adventures we watched. Or rather not her herself, but her image.

Now, instead of Gilgamesh, Enkidu, Hera, and Aphrodite we have the gods of hip-hop, football, music, and cinema. We watch their loves, marriages, divorces, fights, jealousies, and murders, just as we watched those of the gods and goddesses. Angelina Jolie was like Artemis, the goddess of Ephesus. Though that Artemis had dozens of breasts, Jolie has only two breasts—one of them was removed, but she's still a goddess. The fact that despite all our efforts we couldn't even get near her illustrated this. We can only see images of gods and goddesses.

Because we had permission from the deputy governor, we had the chance to talk to the refugees once the official delegation and the actress had left. Hundreds of tents had been lined up side by side, and in front of them were children with dirty faces. They were covered in mud, but they were smiling and playing children's games as if none of the evils that had befallen them had even happened.

When I entered a tent, it was as if I'd gone even further back in time. A pair of eyes more melancholy than any

I'd ever seen were fixed on me. But what eyes. In those eyes I could see the pain that hundreds of thousands of Ezidi had lived, the memories of so many massacres over the generations. The old people were generally quiet. The men sat in the Eastern manner, with one leg folded under them. They looked as if they'd never trimmed their mustaches, and their faces were reminiscent of the landscape of Lalish. A young girl with short hair stood rocking back and forth, murmuring something unintelligible, her eyes blank. (Later I learned that during a raid, this girl was hit on the head, first with a rifle butt and then with a stone. Her mind was gone after that.) Young women were washing laundry in plastic washtubs in front of the tents. There were washtubs of many colors: yellow, green, orange, pink, but there were no dark-blue washtubs. Among the Ezidi, this was a sacred color, and it was considered a sin to use it in daily life. I thought about how many things were considered sinful in this faith. At first it seemed strange to me, but then I thought about all of our taboos. We had so many meaningless ones, like not clipping fingernails at night, reversing the mirrors or covering them with muslin, muttering "with your permission" when walking over dirty water; not doing laundry on Saturdays, sweeping the house when someone leaves on a journey, not stepping out into the street with your left foot, not eating with your left hand. Not being allowed to play football in some districts, because the Prophet's grandson Hussein was beheaded during the Massacre of Karbala and his head was kicked around. Hanging wild rue on the walls to ward off the evil eye, or throwing salt into fire. Indeed there's what my grandmother used to do, she would say "May the evil eye go up their ass," then scratch her nose and then her backside...

When I thought of these, I realized I was being unfair to the Ezidi. But still, romaine lettuce being a sin is really strange.

I asked for the most knowledgeable man in the camp, and they sent me to Sheikh Seyda. I went to his tent. In the Eastern manner, I took this old man's hand, which looked like a tree branch, kissed it and brought it to my forehead. He was clearly in a desperate situation. They thought I was a callous "newspaperman from Istanbul," and it pleased him that I showed respect by kissing his hand. "Sheikh Seyda is the most knowledgeable of the children of *kalam*," they said, "there's nothing he doesn't know. But don't make the mistake of saying 'Satan.' If they hear that they'll stop talking, they won't open their mouths even under threat of death." This word was considered the greatest possible insult to the Peacock Angel.

I asked Seyda the question I was most curious about: Why a peacock? Why did the greatest of the angels take the form of a peacock? Since it's such an old religion, was the peacock always sacred in the Middle East? Seyda began explaining in a low voice. I realized I had to be careful even when I asked questions, because I didn't want to reveal my ignorance.

"That's a difficult question," Seyda said, and then he began to explain. "The Ezidi religion is one of the oldest religions of the East, but in our region, around here, in Lalish, in the Middle East, there are no peacocks, peacocks are from India. This is proof that the Ezidi have their roots in India."

This brought me to my senses. I realized that this poor old man, sitting on a cloth on the dirt floor, really did know a lot, and I felt even more respect. The knowledge of the East is not transmitted through books, as in the West, it's transmitted through the spoken word, through poetry, legends. This was what Seyda was doing, and he spoke of the legends of Zarathustra, the Avesta, Nebuchadnezzar, and Harun al-Rashid as if he'd been alive at the time. He said that Noah's flood occurred a thousand years before Gilgamesh, then he drew a round figure in the dirt in front of him and said Noah's ark was like this, it was round. He went from Sumerian mythology to the legend of a child born without a father to the Zoroastrians, then to the Anatolian minstrels who sang *No one knows this secret / only a Mary knows the truth.* To him, everything was a continuation of everything else, and the same legends were repeated in every century.

I asked him why, if there are faiths in every corner of the world, those that emerged from the Middle East had spread throughout the world. Did we commit the most sins, were we in more need of salvation than anyone else?

I detected a faint smile beneath his grizzly moustache. The answer to this is *kalam,* he said, the word. In this world nothing affects people as much as the word. The Middle East is where the word reached its zenith—no other region's poetry, legends, or fairy tales are as powerful, none other have this much power to influence the human heart. That's why the poets here are classified as magicians. Because people are enchanted by beautiful words.

Then he started reciting couplets in ancient Chaldean, Assyrian, Ezidi, Kurdish, Arabic, Persian, and a number of languages I didn't understand. I felt my admiration for this man increasing steadily. He even knew languages that had disappeared, that had been lost. I dared to ask what made the Peacock Angel different from the other angels. "Because," he said, "he contains both good and evil, just like people. Good and evil stand side by side within every person. Whichever one is nourished becomes the victor. Aren't the gods in other religions like that too? Those are gods that both reward and punish, like the god of the great religions. Could a god who says 'If you don't believe in me I'll pour molten lead down your throat' be only good, my son? Could you call a god who threatens his creatures with the most terrible torture good? Let me tell you a story: in your religion of Islam, a female saint took a bucket of water in one hand and a bucket of fire in the other and set out on a journey. Wherever she went, when people asked her where she was going, she said she was going to quench the fires of hell with one bucket and set heaven on fire with the other. Because she didn't want people to pay lip service simply because of the promise of heaven and the fear of hell. We Ezidi believe there's a place beyond good and evil."

In the mystical atmosphere into which I'd been dragged, when the sheikh said this I suddenly thought of Rumi. As far as I remember he said the following:

There is a place
Beyond good and evil
I'll meet you there

The Sufis spoke of the same thing. I asked the sheikh about their holy books. Do you have a book like the Torah, the Bible, or the Koran, that is, do you have a sacred book? There's the Mushafi Resh, he said. That is, the Black Book. We also have the Mushafi Jelve, a book of revelations, but these aren't the real book, they explain certain customs. Our true holy book is missing. It's memorized and passed down from father to son and from mother to daughter. That's why they call us the children of *kalam*, that is, children of the word.

He smiled. "That is, we're the people of the word." Then he added, "My son the newspaperman, write all of this so that people can learn the truth. We have no connection with Caliph Yezid, who killed Mohammed's grandson Hussein bin Ali. Our god is Ezd."

I promised him I would write everything. But at the same time I had doubts that my editor (who had no interest in this mystical world—his attention was focused on politicians in Ankara and celebrities posing half-naked in Bodrum) would find this subject interesting enough to print. Of course I didn't tell him this. If all else fails, I'll publish it on the internet, I told him, I'll have more freedom.

Perhaps it was impolite, since it might seem as if I wanted something in return for this promise, but I asked him a favor. I said I was looking for a girl named Meleknaz who had come from Syria, a girl from Lalish who had a blind baby. Of course I wasn't expecting him to know her among ten thousand people, but maybe he could help. He thought for a moment, then turned to a young Ezidi man in the tent and said something in Kurdish. The young man bowed slightly with respect, put his right hand over his heart, and said *ser serê min şeyh*. Then the sheikh turned to me. He said that this young man was his son, Shems: "He's going to help you find that girl."

BEYOND RİGHT AND WRONG

As I said before, I'd become caught up in the mystical and extraordinary world of beliefs, and one thing after another was happening. It was impossible there were this many coincidences, and it was making my brain hurt. The day after I spoke to the sheikh, I opened our newspaper, and the picture Hakan had taken of Angelina Jolie and my made-up story (as journalists would say, I had "whipped it up") was in the lower right-hand corner of the front page. So far everything was normal, there was no mystical side to it, but the newspaper had put a picture of her husband, Brad Pitt, next to her picture. A close shot that showed both his face and his arm. Above it was the caption "Brad Pitt had Rumi's poem tattooed on his arm." That was old news, but because of Jolie's arrival they ran it again. Why would Brad Pitt scratch a thirteenth-century

Turkish-Persian poet's verses on his arm? But in this photograph, which had been taken in New Orleans, he was wearing a white, short-sleeved T-shirt and you could see the verse tattooed on his bicep. *There exists a field, beyond all notions of right and wrong. I will meet you there.* Pitt was playing ball with another famous actor on the balcony of a hotel in New Orleans. To tell the truth, this seemed like too much of a coincidence. The words I'd spoken to an Ezidi sheikh just a day earlier were suddenly appearing again in New Orleans. And on the arm of the husband of the angel who had visited the Ezidi camp. I felt as if there were butterflies fluttering around me, as if angels were dancing around me. In fact I'd remembered the verse saying "good and evil," but when it was translated into English it became "beyond right and wrong."

I was getting confused; I didn't know why the tattooed lower lips of the women of Mardin, Brad Pitt's purple tattoo, Rumi's good and evil, the Peacock Angel, and an Assyrian priest were spinning around me, but I had a sensation of spinning endlessly like a fan. Perhaps I was getting ill. I had a headache and my stomach was churning. I kept asking myself what was going on. I didn't know if I was hung over from all the wine I'd drunk out of a water glass in my hotel room, or if it was because of what I'd felt when I saw that woman in the refugee camp. It was probably the latter, because I was already feeling unwell when I got back to the hotel. In the camp we went from tent to tent asking if there was anyone who knew Meleknaz. If the sheikh's son hadn't been with me they wouldn't have allowed me to wander around like that, to go into the tents and ask questions, but everything changed when the sheikh was mentioned. According to what I learned later, the Ezidi have a rigid caste system. The sheikh's commands were always obeyed.

I don't remember whether it was the fifth or the sixth tent, but there was a young woman in a green sweater who knew a Meleknaz who had a blind baby. Her name was Zilan. She had a long, thin face, I thought she might be about twenty, but she turned out to be younger. At first she didn't want to speak, but when the sheikh's son said something to her she told me their stories and I got sick, I really got sick. I was overwhelmed by what Zilan told me. When I rushed out of the camp I was seized by trembling, indeed I threw up a little.

Hakan asked what had happened to me. I said I was fine, come on, let's get back to the hotel. He still insisted on asking me what had happened. "Hakan," I said, "my head hurts and my stomach is churning." I wasn't lying, my temples were really throbbing. It wasn't just about my headache and my upset stomach, but it was part of the truth.

Hakan kept quiet for a while, but then he couldn't contain himself. "Come on, man," he said, "I'm really curious, do these people really worship Satan?"

"No, Hakan," I said, "Satan worships them."

"Really?" he said, and I said, "No, I was just joking, they worship a peacock." I think he was even more surprised by this.

The moment I got back to my room I filled a water glass with wine and downed the whole thing, I filled it again and drank it as if it were water. Then I went and closed the curtains so as not to see the moon, which was shining like a cold, distant, cruel Mesopotamian goddess, and threw myself onto the bed.

ZİLAN'S STORY: THE WATER OF TWO RIVERS COULDN'T WASH IT OFF

"I don't know what to say about it, I don't know what to tell, where to start, where to end; things that can't be spoken of can only be heard by the heart, not by the ear. There is no pain greater than ours, there's no lament greater than ours. Our sorrow is as great as Mount Shingal. They sat on our chests. So much of our blood was shed that the water of two rivers couldn't wash it off. Even the Great Euphrates and the Great Tigris couldn't clean this stain. Oh, oh, oh. Our hearth has been extinguished, our arm has been cut off, owls have roosted on our homes, our story is a story of doom."

Another woman in the tent said this. She was going to continue, but the young man who'd brought me there silenced her with a gesture.

Zilan began telling her story in a dry, flat tone that carried not even the slightest trace of emotion, as if she was performing a duty. She had a thin face, and her cheeks were hollow. She was dark, and her eyebrows met.

"Meleknaz and I are from the same village. Both of us were fifteen years old. We went to school, and sometimes our elders would bring us to Shingal. Shingal was very beautiful, the world was very beautiful, and people were very beautiful. On Red Wednesday, the holiday that marks the creation of the world, we would dye eggs and have a lot of fun. Meleknaz and I would hold hands and wander the streets.

"Meleknaz carried a great secret: her father had made her memorize the lost book. These words carry the ancient knowledge of the Ezidi, around whom the Peacock Angel had drawn a circle, choosing us from among all other peoples, and these words had been written on Meleknaz's mind. Only a few families are entrusted with this. They pass it down from generation to generation, and those families possess the word. Meleknaz was from one of those families.

"That day, bearded men raided our village. They blocked the roads with cars. They gathered all of us in the village square, with women and children on one side and men on the other. They were carrying big weapons, they were all dressed in black, there were black flags hanging from their cars.

"Our men have long moustaches, they never trim them. First they cut off our men's moustaches, and as they did so they shouted that we Ezidi were unbelievers, that we were enemies of Islam. When Uncle Haydar resisted, they took out their knives and cut off his head and rolled it on the ground until it was covered in dirt. I covered Meleknaz's eyes with my hand; she was squeezing my hand so hard I thought it would break. That day they killed three more men, then they loaded the rest into trucks and took them away. My father, my uncle, my brothers, all of them were looking at us from the trucks. We never saw them again.

"Then they loaded us into trucks. They brought us to a city, and they left us in the basement of a large building. They didn't give us bread or water. The whole way, Meleknaz wept for her father and her brothers. Toward evening the next day the bearded men came back. They separated the young girls from their mothers and aunts. They dragged us away by force; we pleaded with them but they didn't pay any attention, they didn't listen. They loaded all the girls between eight and eighteen into a truck again and brought us to another building. Once again Meleknaz was holding my hand tightly; she was trembling. We were tossed into a dim basement. A bit later they gave us water and something to eat. We ate because we no longer had the strength to resist. Then the bearded men started looking at us as if we were merchandise. Some of them touched us everywhere, and they groped us; then they took whichever girl they wanted and left. One man tore my eight-year-old sister from my arms and took her. I threw myself at his feet and pleaded, but he just kicked me and said 'Get away from me, unbeliever.' My sister was crying to me for help.

There was nothing I could do. Then they groped the rest of us and took us away. That day all of us were brought somewhere. The one who took me was forty years old. His upper lip was shaved but he had a long, thick beard, and he always carried a weapon. He brought me home. There were four other women in the house, and his daughter. Everyone was terrified. The man pushed me toward one of the women and said 'Clean this unbeliever up well, I'm going to turn her into a Muslim.' Then he laughed.

"The woman didn't speak, she didn't say anything at all. She just washed me, scrubbed me, and poured hot water over me. Then she gave me a clean robe.

"The man did what he wanted with me that night, but my mind was elsewhere. When I thought about how the same thing was happening to my eight-year-old Nergis I forgot about my own troubles. I found out later they did the same thing to her, and then they beat her because she was crying."

Zilan spoke in an emotionless tone, as if she was reading the weather report. There was no expression whatsoever on her face, there was no inflection in her voice as she talked, and her manner terrified me. I began to picture the events she was relating in such a dry tone, as if my mind was completing what she left unsaid. Who knows what the man who used her looked like? In accounts like this the smell is always left out, though it's one of the most horrible details. The smells must have been so alien for Zilan. The smell of the skin of the man on top of her, the smell of the house, the smell of the man's mouth...

"The man used me for a few days and then sold me to someone else like a pack of cigarettes. They told me that when I'd been in the beds of ten fighters I would be a Muslim. They passed me around for nearly a year. They beat me, and they raped me in every manner. One day I gathered my courage and asked an older man who had bought me, since he seemed a bit more compassionate than the others, wasn't what they were doing a sin? No, he said, this is what our caliph ordained. So, are they doing the same thing to little girls? I asked, because I was still thinking about Nergis. The man took out a paper and read the caliph's decrees. It said that if the girl was developed it was permissible to penetrate her, but if she was not developed, it was permissible to pursue all kinds of pleasure except penetration. Then I said, 'Oh no, Negris is gone. She was eight years old but she was very pretty.' The man continued reading. He said it was permissible to buy two sisters, but it was forbidden to sleep with both of them at the same time. They wrote all of this in a book.

"Then I pleaded with the man. If he found my Negris and bought her I would be his devoted slave; I threw myself at his feet, I begged him. The man laughed. 'You're already my slave,' he said, 'How could you be any more of a slave?' I'll be your slave not just in body, I said, but in soul and heart, bring my sister to me, she's so little, who knows how terrified she's been. I'll become a Muslim, I'll perform my prayers, I'll do whatever you ask.

"The man was kind, he said he'd think about it. I was obedient. Every day when he came home I washed his feet, and when his back hurt I made a balm I'm learned from my grandmother and smeared it on. I even went as far as forcing myself to smile, I tried not to cry when he took me.

"About ten days passed, and the man came home with a girl in a burqa. When he removed the burqa I recognized Nergis. Or rather I both recognized and didn't recognize her. She'd changed. My Nergis was gone, she'd been replaced by someone with a hostile, savage expression. My Nergis, I said, my dearest Nergis... I embraced her, but she didn't return my embrace, she just stood there with her arms hanging by her sides. What happened to you, my child, I asked. She didn't answer. There was a dark hatred in her eyes—she even looked at me like that. When people lose some of their hope, they look sad, but when they're completely without hope they look like this.

"I know because I saw the same thing in Meleknaz. You can't even trust your sister or your parents, you see everyone in human form as a monster, you can't see anything else. I thought it would pass. I was as tender with her as I could be. I hugged her, I kissed her beautiful face, I talked about our parents and the old days, I called her 'Mount Shingal gazelle,' that's what our mother used to call her. I wove her hair into two braids. She didn't utter a single word. That evening the man took her to his room. I listened, but all I heard were the sounds the man made. The next morning the man said my sister had been a waste of money. He'd bought a corpse: 'I got no pleasure from her, I'm going to sell her.' Then I begged him to sell us together, don't separate us, after all, we don't know where our parents and siblings are or what happened to them, don't separate the two of us. The man looked me in the face for a long time, then he said, you're an unbeliever but you're a good girl. Don't wait for them, they're all dead, don't wait in vain, there's nobody left.

"I wept bitter tears; I cried out. Where are you, my beautiful mother, where are you, my mountain-lion father? There was no gravestone beside which I could weep. I wept a flood of tears. The man got tired of this. He said he didn't like women who wept like this. In any event, he'd already had his fill of me, and there were always new girls coming. He was buying younger and younger girls. He agreed to sell Nergis and me together. The following day he sent us to the slave market in Mosul."

THE CRUEL MOONLIGHT

In that bleak hotel room, staring at the light of the cruel and merciless Mesopotamian moon that seeped brazenly past the curtains, I thought about what Zilan had said. Even now I get goosebumps when I think about it. Even though Zilan didn't shed a single tear, she didn't exaggerate anything. She spoke in an ordinary, unexcited, soft, humdrum Arabic, as if she had been talking about cooking, or braiding hair. No, no, that's not quite right, I have to say that I was horrified *because* of her manner rather than in spite of it. I have to say about her relating such horrific events as if they were such natural occurrences...at first I couldn't perceive what this thin, quiet woman was telling me in such calm expressionless manner. It was only when I thought about it afterward that I began to shudder.

Perhaps she was like this because she didn't want to get carried away and relive the events. She didn't want to open the dirty chest in which she'd buried these memories in a remote corner of her mind. This must have been why she told the story in an emotionless manner, as if it was something that had happened to someone else.

One night an ISIS militant of Algerian origin who had come from France opened up to her. He said the reason he'd come there was girls like her. The virgins that had been promised in paradise were here. You could raid a village and take as many little girls "with breasts as small as raisins," and on top of that you were performing a good deed. Is there anything in the world better than this, the young militant said to Zilan, who wouldn't want to come here? It's like going to paradise before you die. When Zilan was heedless enough to say that there was no heaven or hell in the Ezidi faith the man beat her. He beat her badly, her nose bled, and then he raped her brutally and sent her to a friend.

I felt ill. I felt as if my stomach was stuck in my throat. I tried to vomit a couple of times but I couldn't manage to, my head was splitting. I was angry at myself, I was angry at the brown curtain that didn't quite cover the window, I was angry at the moonlight that was streaming past the edge of the curtain, I was angry at my ex-wife, I was angry at the newspaper, but mostly I was angry at myself. Why had I asked these questions, why had I learned about this? I know that if she hadn't received specific orders from her sheikh, Zilan would never have opened her mouth, she wouldn't have said anything, she would have just looked at me in silence the way the other women did. She spoke because the sheikh told her to, but I wonder if I did a good thing by bringing those memories back to her?

As I tossed and turned in bed that night, I tried to picture Zilan, Negris, Meleknaz, and the blind baby. Our species has no right to live in this world, destroying the world and each other. It's true that there's a monster in each of us. I thought that if Zilan, Nergis, and Meleknaz and thousands of others had been animals rather than *Homo sapiens*, they wouldn't have suffered the way they did. Seeing ourselves as superior to plants and animals is an illusion. How base it is of us to exalt humanity.

I also asked myself what the gods of all these different religions were doing while all of this was happening, and I found the answer. God was resting then, because it was the seventh day. He created the universe in six days; then on the seventh day he withdrew to rest. I suppose that's why he didn't hear the screams.

I felt a deep disquiet. It was different from the disquiet I'd felt in Istanbul. This was a new disquiet. It was almost the opposite, but disquiet is such a basic part of life. Peace is rare and fleeting.

That day Zilan told me about the slave market in Mosul, about the various moldy, run-down rooms where they kept the little girls, the young women, and the young boys. They separated the newcomers into different price categories. The first class (that is, the most expensive ones) was young, beautiful, fair-skinned virgins. They kept them in a separate room. The second category was virgin boys and girls.

Children of all ages looked around in confusion, Zilan told me that they didn't know what was going to happen to them. Most of them were crying for their mothers; they beat the children when they did that. The third price category was for those who had been "used up," who were either pregnant or a little older. Zilan was in this category, and she succeeded in keeping Nergis with her by saying she was very "used up."

For three days they were kept in a filthy room and only given enough food and water to stay alive. From time to time some frightful-looking men would come and look at them. They felt them up, they sniffed to see if their breath smelled, they tried to see how "used up" they were by feeling whether their breasts sagged. The men who sold them had no patience with crying or sullenness. They ordered them to smile at the customers. Anyone who didn't was beaten. Nergis had been beaten often for this, but she never said a word. She didn't smile, and the hatred never left her eyes. That's why, even though girls her age were highly prized, she didn't get many customers—they were spooked by the look in her eyes. As for Zilan, she was already in the "used up" category.

As young and attractive virgins came and went, they remained unsold, but three days later something interesting happened. They brought a number of other women to the room. One of them was very pregnant under her burqa, and she was having difficulty moving.

Zilan thought she was going to give birth right there. When the women uncovered their faces, she saw that the pregnant woman was Meleknaz. She went and embraced her. They both started crying; they cried under the indifferent gazes of Nergis and the other women, until the slave master came.

Is that what happened? I wondered whether it was true, or whether I was making these scenes up. Zilan didn't talk about the emotional dimensions, she didn't speak about crying, she just said in the same emotionless tone that the pregnant Meleknaz's face seemed to have aged. Perhaps my mind didn't grasp the concept of "moving beyond the pain," and that's why it kept creating these scenes.

If the reunion between these two women after they'd been torn from each other, after all they'd been through, had been merely an exchange of ice-cold glances, it would have gone against all of my concepts of what makes us human, but perhaps that's really how it happened, how should I know?

A few days later a large, imposing man came. He had a grizzly beard and a grizzly moustache. He asked them questions. He asked their names and where they were from, and then he asked for Zilan. He asked how much she cost. He said he didn't think she was worth it but he might buy her anyway. When the slave merchant asked twenty dollars the man complained: There are fresh, pretty girls for twenty dollars, why would he pay so much for this one? The slave merchant admitted the man was right, but said, "She has a sister, look, what a beautiful girl she is, but she's not untouched. I'll give you both of them for twenty-five dollars."

The man looked at Nergis. He didn't touch her, he just looked, then he looked up and said no, it was too much money. When Zilan saw that the slave merchant was starting to squirm, she interjected, she pointed to Meleknaz and said, "There's this bride too, buy all three of us." The slave merchant liked this idea and looked hopefully at the old man. The man asked what the hell he was going to do with a pregnant woman, all of them are used up, how many hands have they been through, they're living corpses, and one of them is about to give birth. At any other time, Zilan wouldn't have had the courage to speak, but because the slave merchant had been pleased by what she'd said she tried again. "You'll be buying four people for the price of one, uncle," she said. The man said no, where did four people come from? Zilan pointed to Meleknaz's belly and said that when the baby is born it will be worth money. Then the slave merchant and the old man went outside. They bargained a bit, and while she couldn't hear what they were saying it was clear they were arguing. A while later the slave merchant came back in. Come on, he said, you've been sold, get out. So Zilan, Meleknaz, and Nergis stepped out into the sunlight.

The old man was waiting for them in a green pickup truck. The three of them got into the back; they drove for quite some time. Zilan saw men walking on the street through the slit in her burqa. Then the man stopped in front of a shop, and he went in without saying anything to them. A while later he came out with a number of bags. He gave the girls a large bottle of water, and they set off again. They traveled for hours along dusty roads. They were stopped a few times at checkpoints; the man showed them his papers and said something to them.

They bounced along like that until evening. As the sun was setting the truck stopped on the slope of a hill, where there was a nearby stream. The old man told them to get out of the truck. They helped Meleknaz get down. When Zilan saw that deserted hillside she supposed that the man was going to kill them there. Until then the man had only spoken Arabic, but now he suddenly started speaking Kurdish.

"Come on," he said, "let's pray toward the setting sun in the name of the Peacock Angel." With the man in front and the girls behind, they prayed three times toward the sun. Then the man said, "My daughters, don't be afraid, I bought you not to do you harm but to rescue you. I'm Ezidi, but everyone thinks I'm an Arab Muslim. I live among them with a false identity. Beyond this hill is our Shingal, our sacred mountain. From there you can cross to Rojava and reach the Turkish border. If you go on any of the main roads they'll catch you right away. Your only hope is to cross this mountain—take as much food as you can carry. May the Peacock Angel help you, and may our Sheikh Adi ibn Musafir protect you."

Then he just got into his pickup truck and left. There was complete silence: it was as if even the bubbling of the stream couldn't be heard. Without speaking, the three girls opened the bags the man had given them. They ate bread, cheese, and spicy sausage and filled their empty water bottle from the stream. Then they slept.

"Didn't you talk about anything," I asked Zilan. She said no. "You didn't even exchange a word?" I asked. She said no. "So weren't you frightened?" I asked.

"I was frightened, she said. "I don't know about the others, but I was frightened more for Negris and the pregnant Meleknaz than I was for myself. I was worried about how we were going to climb the mountain with that load."

THE MOUNTAIN

"Mighty Shingal Mountain, shelter and savior of the Ezidi, the miracle of Adi ibn Musafir, we've come to you, we've taken shelter in you, protect us, protect Nergis, protect the little child in Meleknaz's belly. I prayed so much that you would take us into the shadow of your wings, but on the mountain there was no shade, there were no trees, there was no water. We were covered in dust as we climbed, we closed our burqas to protect ourselves from the dust, our black burqas became white from the dust, we were out of breath. The sacred sun sent down blind fire as if it wanted to burn and roast us. We each took one of Meleknaz's arms as we struggled along. There were other Ezidi walking on the mountain, but no one had the strength to look up and see anyone else. We looked for shade at the base of the rocks and we sheltered there. We saw a small child behind one rock; he'd died of thirst. I suppose his family had continued on. The child was just lying there; his lips were cracked, his mouth hanging open. We lay down next to him because it was shady there.

"Meleknaz was having a lot of difficulty. I worried that she wouldn't have the strength to climb the mountain, but she gave it everything she had. She put her hand on her aching back and tried to catch her breath, and then she started climbing again. We sipped at the water in the bottle we'd filled from the stream. We slept by day and walked by night. We heard gunfire in the distance, explosions, bombs, artillery. We hid in fear that they were coming after us. Foul smells wafted to us from the bottom of a ravine. We saw Ezidi families, children, young people and old people, who had succumbed. They'd embraced one another as they were dying. We supposed they'd died of hunger. We prayed for them, we had no strength left, we lay down next to the dead bodies.

"There was moonlight that night. The rocks were glowing, Meleknaz was having contractions, and her water broke. I laid her down in a cavity in the rocks. She didn't cry out because she was afraid she would be heard. She just moaned. She writhed for about two hours, and then the baby started to come, I helped her the way I'd seen the elders do in our village. I became the baby's midwife, I cut the umbilical cord with a stone, then I ripped up our black burqas and swaddled the baby. As I cleaned Meleknaz up, I said to her, 'Congratulations, you have a daughter, may the Peacock Angel help you, may the seven angels protect her. A baby was born among all of these dead bodies; a new life has come into the world.' She started crying. I handed the baby to Meleknaz. I wanted her to hold the baby, but she didn't even look at her. She turned her head away and gestured for me to take it away.

"Nergis was already in a different world. She wasn't at all interested in the baby, she was looking at the dead bodies, she was looking at their frozen faces in the moonlight. She rocked back and forth on her feet without making a sound.

"The baby was crying, of course, I took her in my arms and rocked her. There were dangerous men around, and I was afraid they would hear the baby's cries and find us, but the baby kept crying. 'Meleknaz,' I said, 'if you don't give this baby your breast it won't stop crying, please don't do this, don't put us all in danger.' She took the baby in her arms. At first no milk came, but the hungry baby kept sucking with all her strength. Then the milk came, and the baby drank her fill. I took her in my arms again. I rocked her to sleep, and we slept a little despite our hunger and thirst.

"We spent the day there, and we set off again in the evening. I carried the baby, and when she cried I gave her to Meleknaz to suckle. She allowed the baby to suckle without saying a word, but she didn't look at the baby's face. Then it happened. It happened at the least expected moment."

Here Zilan stopped. Her face went pale, and when I asked her to continue she said she would prefer not to.

When I asked her to please continue she looked at me with hatred. In her eyes I could see the hatred she felt for the cruel man who was making her speak of these things.

"I woke one morning to find that Nergis was missing. We were on top of a peak. I looked everywhere for her, and then I saw her at the bottom of a cliff down below. She'd thrown herself over the edge, I rolled down toward her, rocks and thorns piercing me all over. I crawled toward her—she was still alive, but her legs and arms were broken. When I took her in my arms I saw that her head was wet with blood. She opened her eyes, and she spoke to me for the first time since I'd seen her. 'I was a human being, Sister,' she said. These were her last words; she didn't say anything more. I wanted to bury her little body, but the ground was very stony, and there was no soil. If there had been I would have dug with my fingernails. There was nothing I could do but gather stones and pile them on top of her. I turned to the sun and prayed. I commended Nergis to the mercy of the Peacock Angel, and then I climbed back up to Meleknaz. I told her what had happened. We entrusted Nergis to the sacred Shingal Mountain, and then we continued on our way.

"Meleknaz would take time to suckle the baby, then she would give her to me. We were hungry, we were thirsty, we were exhausted, we were having difficulty carrying the baby, and besides, Meleknaz didn't want the baby. Once she left the baby to die at the base of a rock, but after walking for an hour she couldn't bear it. She went back, she gave the baby milk as she rested in the shadow of that rock. For several days we'd been picking herbs and grasses—we were grazing on sweet and bitter herbs like cattle. One day Meleknaz told me to come, and she put her left breast in my mouth; she suckled me. The milk was warm, it was very sweet, it was mother's milk, it was sweet. Meleknaz became my mother, she was feeding me. That milk was like the water of life to me. Then she wanted me to cup my hands, so I did. Meleknaz squeezed her right breast and squirted milk into my cupped hands, and then she leaned down and drank it. That milk kept us alive.

"Then I told Meleknaz that we had to name the baby. An Ezidi baby must have a name, it would be a sin not to name her. I asked her what name she wanted to give the baby. She said she didn't know, it was none of her business. It doesn't matter who the father was, the baby isn't at fault, she's a life. After so many rapes there was no way to know who the father was. I told her that this baby had come to her as a gift from the Peacock, and look, she saved both of our lives, your milk is keeping us alive.

"I asked if we could name her Nergis, and she agreed. We gave the name of the Nergis we'd left in Shingal to the baby who was born in Shingal. The next day I realized that the baby was blind. There was a white film covering her eyes, and she couldn't see anything. Later, the doctors at the camp said that stress and illness during pregnancy could lead to complications like this. At the very moment we'd almost completely run out of strength, some armed people appeared from behind a hill. There were three of them. They had rifles slung over their shoulders, and as they approached we saw that all three of them were girls. They were dark, wiry girls, seventeen or eighteen years old at the most. They asked who we were, and when they learned we were Ezidi they helped us, they gave us water, they gave us bread, and then they went in the direction we'd come from. They said they were going to kill the people who'd made us suffer so much. There were sounds of gunfire coming from that direction.

"Descending the far side of the mountain was easier. We had water, bread, and milk, and it was easier than climbing. When we reached the bottom and crossed into Rojava, people greeted us. They brought us to a village, they fed us and cleaned us, and they brought us across to Turkey at a place called Qamishli. Then the Turks settled us into a camp, where we were seen by doctors. That's it, that's the whole story."

THIS WORLD IS A WINDOW: EVERY PASSERBY LOOKS THROUGH IT, THEN MOVES ON

As I was passing a shop the next day in Mardin, I heard a voice singing a folk song. The jeweler inside was singing an ancient folksong as he made filigree. I knew the tune, but that day I paid attention to the lyrics for the first time: The man sang in a poignant voice, *This world is a window / Every passerby looks through it, then moves on.* That's right, I thought, that's right. I'm not interested in philosophy or anything. You know those people who philosophize as if they're in a coffeehouse? I get annoyed by people who talk about things like the meaning of life, and recently it's begun to make me even more angry.

I'm angry at all of the philosophers, poets, prophets, and saints. I wonder why all of those books were written? What need was there for those pamphlets, those conferences, those meetings? Those politicians who think they're really something? Journalists like me, the serious expressions of the know-it-alls who appear on the screen and talk as if they're going to save the world, universities, those people who talk about themselves as if they're something? If they gathered us all together we wouldn't amount to more than a fig seed. Especially the wealthy, especially the money, especially that extravagance. I thought all of them should be buried with their showy watches, diamond rings, and limousines. Heaven forbid they be separated from those things. The song I heard the jeweler sing as I passed his shop got stuck in my head: I kept repeating, *This world is a window / Every passerby looks through it, then moves on.*

What else is this but philosophy? Enough books to collapse a bookshelf, all of those universities, those high-and-mighty philosophy professors, can those who supposedly questioned existence say anything other than this? Or those who make their living as religious scholars? Do all the words of those who buy and sell religion say anything other than this? Everything they say is explained by these two lines from a Black Sea folk song. *This world is a false world / The next world is doubtful.*

After talking to Zilan, everything I saw seemed like nonsense. I don't know how to explain it. Whatever I did, whether I was walking, talking, eating, all of the things I normally did, I felt a sense of emptiness. As if there was a deep nothingness within me.

I wrote this to try to fill that void. I might get a book out of it, but I have to admit I don't know what the purpose of this is. What difference would it make if I wrote it? What would change if people read it, what would change if people didn't read it? This had been my state of mind since the day I listened to Zilan. I often thought of Nergis lying under the rocks on Mount Shingal, and I decided that I had a single purpose in this life. One purpose, one single purpose: to find the girl called Meleknaz, to talk to her. As if she was the only person who could fill the void that was opening within me. As I wrote and wrote, I found the answer to why I was writing this book: my aim wasn't to inform the world about what happened, to shake the world by showing people—Angelina Jolie could do that kind of thing far better than I. I wrote just to heal myself, to find the strength to live among so-called human beings again. Or at least that's what I thought. I was writing to free myself from the *harese* that had taken people in its claws, that left blood in everyone's mouth as if we were desert camels, and from time to time I repeated those words to myself: "I was a human being!"

Mardin's narrow little streets, the stone buildings, the dust of time and the atmosphere of a lost world were beginning to suffocate me, and the distress within me was growing. I wanted to flee this city where time flowed backward. I wanted to return to the twenty-first century, but there were two things I had to do before I left: to learn what had happened to Hussein and to find Meleknaz's trail.

The first task was easy, but the second was difficult. The people I spoke to at the camp didn't know where the girl was either. They spoke of Hussein lovingly; they kept talking about what a good-hearted, charitable, wonderful man he was. They were deeply saddened to learn of his death, and they mourned him for days, but all they knew was that this good man had fallen in love with Meleknaz, that he'd asked the camp authorities for permission to marry her and that he'd taken her away.

Before she left the camp she embraced Zilan, swore to her that as soon as she'd established a home she was going to bring her there and they would live together. Then she picked up her blind baby and left. This was all they knew. I had no idea how I was going to find this girl, and in the end I told myself that if anyone knew it would be Aysel. The following day I went to that house of mourning and knocked on the blue door that was almost completely covered in romaine lettuce.

You know how they say the blind man asked Allah for one eye and was given two? That day luck was on my side. Not only was Aysel home, but so was her older brother, Salim, who was going to return to Germany the following day. The two siblings were drinking their morning coffee from silver-sleeved cups, and I joined them. Aysel was wearing a black headscarf because she'd cut off her two waist-length braids and thrown them into the grave. She also wore it as a mark of mourning. I told Aysel that I would be leaving Mardin within the next two days, but I didn't want to leave before learning what had happened to Hussein: "To write what I'm writing, I need to know everything in order to keep his memory alive. You're grieving, I respect that, but I beg you to please tell me, what happened after Hussein found that girl at the monastery?"

Salim was much older than us, so I only had vague memories of him from childhood. He inhaled deeply from his cigarette and watched us with a troubled, distressed expression.

Aysel said, "Did you see the old, yellow Opel parked near the door, I mean that pile of junk with one of the bumpers about to fall off? That was my late brother's car. When he found the girl sheltering in the monastery, he put her in his car and wanted to bring her straight back to our house. The girl insisted she wouldn't go, she couldn't go. He promised that there would be no romaine lettuce in the house, no matter how he thought he was going to keep that promise. But when they pulled up in front of the house and she saw the romaine hanging on the door, she closed her eyes and turned her back. She refused to get out of the car. After the girl fled the house, my mother didn't just hang romaine on the door, she hastily painted it blue. She recited the entire Koran to keep Satan away from the house. My mother was so terrified, she was almost beside herself as she struggled to ward off that evil. Now she keeps saying, see, I was right, that she-devil consumed my lion-hearted son. She rarely leaves her room. She spends her days in prayer and supplication, and reading the Koran.

"When my brother couldn't bring the girl in, he came in himself. I was the one who answered the door. I asked him to come in, but my mother shouted to him not to come in, don't you dare come in! My brother was taken aback by this. He understood about the girl, but was his mother kicking him out of the house? Mother, he said, are you refusing to allow me into my father's house? My mother said, no, my son, you're the apple of my eye, but if you've touched that girl, if you've spoken to her, don't come into the house unless you've performed your ablutions. My brother tried to object, he tried to tell her that the girl had done nothing wrong, that she didn't worship Satan, but my mother wouldn't say a word. All she said was, if you consider me to be your mother, you'll do as I say. I washed your diapers with these hands, I still have your shit under my fingernails. I don't want all my efforts to have been for nothing.

"Then my brother was in a desperate state. He'd always been my mother's favorite. He heaved such a deep sigh that my heart ached, and then he asked us to just give him the baby, so he could bring her to her mother. The poor baby was sleeping. I'd grown very fond of her; my heart ached when I looked at her. I took her in my arms, went to the door, and gave her to my brother. I asked him what the baby's name was, and he said Nergis. 'What a beautiful name this unfortunate child has,' I said, but my mother got angry at this. My brother gave the baby to the girl, and then he started the car and sped off. My mother didn't let anything show, but I was afraid my brother would never come back. Anyway, it didn't turn out as I feared. He came in the evening: 'Don't worry, Mother, the girl is gone, I performed my ablutions in the mosque courtyard, are you happy now?'

"'I'm happy now,' said my mother, and she went and embraced him. 'Bless you, my Hussein, you were always a good son, you didn't leave me and go to the other end of the world like my other two sons,' she said as she stroked my brother's hair. That evening at dinner my mother was very cheerful. She couldn't ask, but she wanted to believe that my brother had brought the girl back to the camp and left her there, that he was on the right path again. She even started making plans for getting him back together with Safiye. She was going to tell her that things like this happen when you're young, that that she-devil had enchanted her son, but thankfully in the end he was on the right path again. But the situation was different from what she thought, and after my mother went to bed he told me everything.

"He had a close friend from the army who was in Istanbul. He called him and asked if he could put the girl and her baby up for a while. Then he put them on a plane and sent them to Istanbul. His friend and his wife would pick them up at the airport, and they would stay with them until my brother could get to Istanbul—they said they were happy to do this. 'I can't give this girl up,' my brother said to me, 'I can't leave her simply because of mother's nonsense'—I'm sorry, he was talking as if he was completely infatuated. Then I realized that we'd lost my brother completely. I started crying, but of course I had no idea how bad things were going to get.

"My brother stayed in the house for two more days; he took care of some things he had to do. I don't know what it was he had to do, but he took care of it. He said he had debts to pay: I think he was borrowing money to give to the refugees at the camp. (That's how he got into debt. He never spent money on himself, his car was almost a piece of junk—you saw it.) He said goodbye to his friends. I didn't know what he was doing; he left in the morning and came back in the evening, but he didn't come back on the third evening. In fact we thought he'd stayed with friends. We weren't worried at all; he visited his friends frequently, but that wasn't the case.

"In the evening there was a knock on our door, and it was a policeman we knew. 'Your brother isn't so well, Aysel,' he said, 'we brought him to the hospital. Come, I'll take you there.' My mother let out a scream. She grabbed her headscarf and was almost out the door before I was. On the way we kept asking the policeman what had happened, but he didn't really tell us anything, he just mumbled something. When we got to the hospital they told us he was in surgery, and that's when they told us what had happened.

"As my brother was walking home that evening, just as he was passing the mosque, someone dashed toward him out of a side street. He shouted 'Allahu Akbar' and then started shooting at my brother. After my brother fell to the ground he continued shooting. He shouted that this was what happens when you betray Allah for Satan. Then he ran off.

"People heard the gunfire and hurried there. My brother was covered in blood—they rushed him to the hospital. He was in surgery for three hours; for three hours we kept dying and coming back to life. Then a doctor in green scrubs came out of the operating room. He told us he had good news—he'd been hit by two bullets, but no vital organs had been damaged. 'We're going to bring him to intensive care, he should be in a regular room tomorrow,' he said. My mother and I started crying with relief. I wanted to kiss the doctor's hand and bless him, but he wouldn't let me. He was a good man. He filled us in on my brother's condition, he put us at ease, and he even gave us permission to see him from behind the glass in intensive care. My poor brother, his face was ghostly white, there was a tube coming out of his nose, serum was dripping into his arm, he was just lying there. One bullet had hit him in the shoulder, and the other hit his left arm. There were policemen at the hospital too. From what they told us, ISIS militants in Mardin were responsible for the attack. Because he wanted to marry that Yezidi girl, a Yezidi girl who refused to become a Muslim. They could only be concubines, they could only be slaves. They'd found the assailant, a young man named Idris from a village near Mardin. He wasn't sorry about what he'd done. He was only sorry that he hadn't 'bumped him off.' In his statement he said that this man had insulted Islam, and that's why he had to be punished. 'The only punishment for Allah's enemies is death,' he kept saying. 'Anyway, our warriors will finish the job I left undone; no one can stand in our way; the caliphate is Allah's sword of revenge,' he said as he pounded his fists against the bars of his cell. When my mother heard this, she started crying even more. 'We're a Muslim family, my son,' she said to the policeman. 'Our family has many hajjis, many hodjas, my son is a devout young man. Why are they slandering us like this?'

"The policeman tried to calm my mother. 'We know,' he said, 'no one has any doubts about your piety. Thank Allah, we're all Muslims. But if only your son hadn't taken up with that she-devil.' My mother said, 'May that girl be struck blind. Look at all the misfortune she brought us, may she go blind, may her world turn dark, tell those *ishish* people, tell them that Aunt Adviye's son is fully a Muslim, tell them not to harm my child again.'

"My mother always refers to ISIS as *ishish,* and no matter how we tried to correct her she doesn't get it. We spell it out for her, tell her it stands for the Islamic State of Iraq and Syria. That is, ISIS. 'That's what I say, my child, *ishish.*' It always made us laugh when she mispronounced words she'd just learned. She said *mitralyöz* (machine-gun) instead of meteorology, she said *smelf* instead of shelf. She didn't know what ISIS was. 'May Allah show those boys the right path, there's no coercion in our religion, what are they doing going around cutting people's heads off, they should repent.' The religion my mother knew consisted of prayer and fasting, alms and charity, of helping the poor. At her age she can't even conceive anything other than this. She couldn't bring herself to believe that ISIS was beheading people in the name of Islam. She would say that it was all infidel slander, and leave it at that. But when those *ishish* people shot her beloved son they became 'those cursed devils.'

"My brother left the hospital within a week. We took good care of him at home, we made his favorite foods, we made *meftune,* diced lamb with eggplant and tomatoes. We brought the tray to his bed but he didn't eat any of it. He was clearly exhausted, and this pained us. My mother put it down to the attack, but I knew that he was suffering from love: being separated from Meleknaz was burning his heart. My dear brother, my beloved brother, I begged him not to do this to himself. At the same time we were terrified. The assailant had said that this wasn't over, that the other fighters would finish him off. My mother had amulets prepared, she had hodjas whose prayers were answered recite the entire Koran. She didn't leave it at that; she had our Assyrian neighbors bring her to church so she could light candles to the Virgin Mary and say a prayer. 'Mother Mary, they did a great evil to your son, only you could understand the state I'm in, I implore you to save my son.' She prayed like this for days. She still believed that everything that had happened to us was because of that girl who worshipped Satan. Mother and I were beside ourselves. Meanwhile my brothers in Germany had heard about what had happened. At first we didn't want to tell them, but they heard from friends and neighbors. Salim was quite angry with us for not telling him. Then he said, 'Since this is the situation, why not send him here? He should just get on a plane as soon as he's well enough to travel. For the love of Allah, don't waste time, he should come at once, the situation is extremely dangerous, I'll send his ticket, we'll get him treatment here, otherwise there's no way we can save him from ISIS. It's certain they'll kill him.'

"My mother was very relieved to hear this. She always used to complain about how her worthless sons had left her alone and moved so far away, but then she began saying prayers for Salim and Abdullah.

"However, it was difficult for Hussein to accept this. He said he couldn't leave Meleknaz and go to Germany—of course he said this to me, not to our mother. I insisted that he should go first, that he could send for her later. 'God forbid that they kill you, then you won't be of any use to Meleknaz and her child.' I said this over and over.

"Salim said that he should apply for a passport right away—that we should get friends and acquaintances to help with the bureaucracy, but we needed to get him a passport as soon as possible—'I'll send him an invitation, that will make it easier for him to get a German visa.' He called every day from some place called Cakson to insist that we begin the process right away. It would be impossible for Meleknaz to leave the country. Since she'd come from Syria as a refugee, it would be impossible for her to leave with the identity papers she'd been given. One day when I was talking to Abdullah I told him that Hussein wouldn't listen to us—'He respects you, please talk to him.' Abdullah and Salim talked to him at length. 'Come here,' they said, 'work with us, we can bring the girl and her baby here later, you can live comfortably here.' Finally they were able to convince the poor man.

"Hussein asked if there was any discrimination against Ezidi there, and they said no. The phone was on speaker; I was listening too. 'This is Germany, everyone lives freely according to their own faith, it's not like it is there, no one interferes with anyone else's religion.' They went on about how it was the land of freedom, and they swore that they would find a way to bring Meleknaz and her child. Indeed they said they would find treatment for the blind baby and make her better. Poor Hussein got his hopes up then. He said fine, he would come.

"We were delighted, though we would miss him terribly, just as we missed our other brothers. My mother and I would be left alone with no man in the house, but as long as he was alive, nothing else was important. Thankfully we got help from our acquaintances and got him a passport. He was able to get a visa too with the letter of invitation my brothers sent, because my brothers had opened a pizza restaurant in that place called Cakson. As far as we'd heard they were doing well, they had a good reputation and a good income. This made it easy for Hussein to get a visa. Meanwhile, even though his arm was still a bit stiff, it was getting better. One day we bade him farewell in tears. My mother poured water after him; she wept as well. Only, as he was leaving, he said something strange: 'You can't protect me any longer, Mother, not even if you took me and put me back in your womb!'

"We didn't understand why he was saying this, and I wondered what had got into him. Then Hussein left. He went to Istanbul first to see the girl, then he went to Germany. Anyway, that's what happened."

GERMANY, GERMANY

As I listened to Aysel, who had tears streaming from her almond eyes, my heart broke. I thought of the story of the poor vizier who traveled from Baghdad to Samarkand to flee the angel of death, but when he arrived the angel of death greeted him and said "I was going to take you here anyway, I'm glad you came, you saved me the trouble of going to Baghdad." Hussein had rushed to Germany for his appointment with Azrael. I only had vague memories of Salim and Abdullah from childhood. They moved to Germany after I left Mardin. First they worked at a pizza place in Köln—they had a difficult time but they learned the business. Then they moved to Duisburg, which has a large Turkish population, and opened their own restaurant. They had both married and had children.

Everyone in Mardin spoke of them enviously. They didn't conceal the envy they felt at imagining them living the kind of Western life they only saw in movies. As if I wasn't envious too, I thought. Was it possible to call the life I was living a life, struggling to get by in the chaos of Istanbul, burying myself every day in news of violence, paying alimony to a harsh and selfish woman (meanwhile, I wondered if they were going to give us a raise this year...sometimes the bosses didn't give us a raise because it was a bad year, and if anyone asked for a raise they told them to get lost, but with unemployment the way it is, they have nowhere to go), being afraid to go to an ATM because a bomb might go off, being hesitant to even go to the movies. I thought about how right Ibn-Khaldūn was, how right he was to say that geography is destiny. While people who were born in America or Europe have happy, healthy lives, our lives are caught up in the *barese* that Uncle Fuat spoke of. We're like camels who bleed when they eat thistles, who continue to eat as we bleed, and who drown in our own blood.

Then I thought of poor Hussein. Perhaps everyone carries their fate within them, I thought. That is, as Cavafy said, "The city will always pursue you." Could Hussein have carried his Middle Eastern fate to Germany?

Mardin was going to drive me out of my mind, the way time flowed backward. This metaphysical world could put even the sanest person into a mystical and alien mood. I told myself that I wasn't thinking straight. I'd lost my ability to think properly, I couldn't separate fable from reality, I kept asking myself strange questions. If there hadn't been a civil war in Syria, if the world hadn't stirred this war up, if ISIS hadn't been able to sell its oil, those terrible things wouldn't have happened to Meleknaz, Zilan, and Nergis. They would have married and had children in their village. Three million refugees would not have come to Turkey, Hussein would never have met Meleknaz, he would have married Safiye and carried on his life in Mardin. If there wasn't so much prejudice in the world, no one would have believed these innocent admirers of a peacock were worshipping Satan...

Of course, thinking these things didn't get me anywhere, but I was seized by an urgent wish to see Meleknaz, as if this would solve everything. And it was difficult for me not to take out that soft handkerchief and touch that black-and-red Peacock Angel.

Salim was a sober, quiet, dignified man who seemed troubled. He'd listened calmly while Aysel was speaking. He didn't interrupt once. I sensed that the years had created a distance between them. It was as if there was a wall of space and time between them. From time to time Aysel gave him a hesitant glance. Perhaps she was secretly blaming him for bringing Hussein there so this could happen to him. Salim was returning to Germany the following day. After bringing his brother back and burying him, there was nothing left for him to do here. I offered to drive him to the airport; I asked him to let me drop him off. After all, the news photographer and I were returning to Istanbul anyway. I wanted to talk to him during the drive. He accepted.

SALIM RECOUNTS

I didn't tell the details to my mother or Aysel. Ibrahim, they wouldn't have been able to take it. Even as a man, when I think about it I feel as if I'm going to lose my mind. What does it mean to smear pig fat on a knife? They cut the poor boy up with a butcher knife, and while they were doing it they shouted that they'd smeared pig fat on it, what kind of insanity is that?

Man. I would never have brought him to Germany if I'd thought something like that would happen. I know you probably don't want me to smoke in the car, Ibrahim, but I can't stand it, I quit when I was in Germany. People don't smoke much there, you know, but after this disaster I started again. We have a small pizza place in Duisburg. Don't imagine that it's some kind of fancy, expensive place, it's in a poor neighborhood. Unfortunately there's a lot of crime, it's an inexpensive place, our customers are mainly from the neighborhood. Sometimes police officers would drop by, and we became friends with some of them. Anyway, they told us the details of what happened.

The two maniacs who killed Hussein, they're in prison now, of course. They were members of a racist, white supremacist group; they were neo-Nazis who hated Blacks, Latinos, and Asians. They have a German name, I can never quite remember it, they're Hitler Youth whose brains have been thoroughly washed, they hate all foreigners, and in recent times they've come to hate Muslims most. They practice shooting in the woods, they sing fascist marches, they train. I've never come across these punks—we'll see their cursed faces in court. We hired a lawyer, and we're going to do everything we can to make sure they get the harshest punishment possible. We never experienced any problems like this. They smashed our windows a couple of times, and once some scrawny student tried to rob us, but our police officer friends helped us take care of these situations.

When Hussein came he stayed with us at first. My wife is German, we have three children. A while later Hussein came to our restaurant. He started working and learning the business. Hussein helped us because he didn't have a work permit. He cleaned the floors and the tables and counters, and then he'd close up the shop and come home. We told him there was no need, that he should concentrate on his German course, and later we'd find him a job in the medical field. We told him we'd get him a work permit, but he didn't listen to us, he insisted on working in the restaurant. At the same time he was working on improving his German. He struggled to speak German with my wife and the children, and when the children laughed at his mistakes he laughed with them good-naturedly. You know what a good-hearted man my brother was, Ibrahim, he was such an angelic boy. When we moved to Germany years ago, there wasn't as much xenophobia as there is now. But these maniacs who plant bombs in the Middle East, the suicide bombers, the killers, they've really stirred things up. We try to tell the people we know that these people have nothing to do with Islam, that they're all mentally ill, but we couldn't even convince our wives. After every terrorist incident we felt a needless sense of guilt, as if we were responsible for those maniacs. Because Ulrike knew me and wanted to console me, she said there were different kinds of Islam, that they weren't all the same, but somehow we weren't able to explain this to anyone else. The scourge of ISIS made things even worse. As Muslims we couldn't bear the way they beheaded American and European journalists, burning that pilot in a cage, and on top of that disseminating videos of these atrocities. They even shot my poor brother. The children are frightened, and we feel a deep disquiet. It's the same here, maybe even worse. There's no place left on earth that's peaceful...

The restaurant did well that evening, and as we were cashing out the register we each had a Kölsch beer to relax. We didn't know what was going to happen. The three of us were in good spirits—indeed that day when he was serving an Algerian customer, the customer asked a question and he tried to answer that there was no *Schweinefleisch* on the pizza, but instead he said there was no *Schwanz*, we laughed at this (the first word meant pork, the second, excuse me, is the word for the male organ). The German customers laughed as well. He said what can I do, I'm Muslim. We told him what he'd said, he blushed and said that next time he would get it right. Then Abdullah and I left together. Hussein stayed, as he did every evening, to mop the floors, wipe the tables, close up the shop, and pull down the shutters before coming home.

When I got home the children were asleep, Ulrike had waited up for me as always. I told her the restaurant was doing more business. The phone rang as I was getting ready for bed. It was the police. They asked if I had a relative named Hussein—he'd been carrying his passport and the restaurant's card, and they'd traced me through the card. Yes, I said, he's my brother, has anything happened? Then it was as if the world had collapsed on top of us. They wanted us to come to the hospital as soon as possible. Ulrike stayed with the children, and I jumped into the car immediately.

I picked up Abdullah on the way, but by the time we got to the hospital it was too late. They showed us our brother's body. The police wanted us to identify him, and to tell the truth it was difficult to see that innocent, snow-white face. All the blood had drained out of it. Both of us started crying. The police, the doctors and the nurses were all kind to us. Some of our acquaintances among the police came too. They brought us to the station to get our statements. We told them everything. They were upset too.

There's something else, I forgot. The doctor in the emergency room—the man was of Indian origin—told us Hussein had said something before he died. The man hadn't understood what he was saying so he recorded it on his cell phone. He played it for us and asked what it meant. Hussein had said "I was a human being" twice; perhaps he said it several times, but that was all that was on the recording. My poor brother said "I was a human being" in a wheezing voice.

Later Abdullah and I talked about this a lot. We didn't understand why he'd said this, using the past tense that way. We went to the restaurant with the police, we looked at the security camera footage. We found out later that they'd looked at footage from all of the cameras in the area, indeed that's how they caught those two men. Despite our insistence they wouldn't let us see the footage, but they told us what happened.

After he closed up the restaurant Hussein headed home along a deserted avenue. Then those two punks came up to him. After saying something to him they each took out a knife and stabbed him in the abdomen, and they kept stabbing him after he fell to the ground. When they made their statements after they were caught, they said they'd seen Hussein in the restaurant—that means the assailants were customers—they knew he was a Muslim, indeed in the restaurant he'd boasted he was Muslim, he was making propaganda. They said they'd wanted to kill him as a lesson to others. Beforehand they'd smeared the knives with pig blood—that's what they said to Hussein; they made fun of him because he wasn't going to be able to go to heaven. They shouted *Schwein, Schwein* as they stabbed him. At the end of their statements they said they didn't regret what they'd done: "We're not at all sorry, we're going to keep fighting until there are no Turks left in Germany." When I think about it, it drives me crazy, Ibrahim, what ISIS left unfinished was finished by fascists who call themselves Volk something or other. I mean, Muslim jihadis and Crusader Nazis committed a joint murder. After committing a murder they put either a crescent or a crucifix around their necks, it doesn't make any difference. Is there anything like this in the world? For the love of God, this strange murder came and found us. If you'd seen the innocent expression on Hussein's face in the morgue, it would have torn you apart. You're a journalist, Ibrahim, you should tell everyone about this, let everyone know what happened to your friend. Please, tell everyone how crazy the world has gone. I'm sorry, brother, my nerves are really shot, I'm giving you a headache and suffocating you with smoke. I made you cough. After what happened to Hussein I've taken refuge in smoke. My wife gets angry at me too, she won't allow me to smoke at home, around the children... Desperation.

journey
to
meleknaz

MERCY IS NOT A BALM FOR CRUELTY

Stupefied by the stories I'd been told, I returned to Istanbul with an ever-growing disquiet. I somehow couldn't pull myself together and focus on my work. It was as if my body had flown to Istanbul, but my soul had remained in Mardin. No matter how I struggled I couldn't free myself from the atmosphere of Mesopotamia. I was like a fly caught in a jar; I'd been captured by the stones and the sun and the smell of spices, by slowly flowing time and the mystery of the desert. Finding Meleknaz, seeing her and talking to her, had become an obsession with me; I thought about her day and night.

I know it sounds like nonsense, but I felt drawn toward this girl I'd never even seen a photograph of. Yes, yes, I was being drawn straight toward her. From time to time I tried to make fun of myself—I laughed and referred to my struggles to find Meleknaz as the "Journey to the Center of Love." But in fact this wasn't love; maybe it was something that had its source in my journalistic curiosity, but I won't lie, at times it went beyond that. Was I turning into Hussein? Nevertheless, this self-mockery didn't work. I felt a disquiet; I couldn't taste anything I ate or drank. Conversations with my friends seemed empty; the work I did at the newspaper seemed senseless. Perhaps I was the only man in the world so drawn to a girl he'd never seen. In old Eastern fairy tales, a white-bearded holy man enters someone's dream and shows him an image of a girl. The fire of love is sparked within him and he spends the rest of his life searching for her... Mine wasn't like that either—I never even saw the girl's face in my dreams. I had no idea what she looked like, but I thought about her day and night. In fact this was a very strange thing. There were none of the pheromones that draw men and women to each other, none of the scents, none of the harmony of skin; no personality, attitude, or behavior; no smiles, no glances, no figure; no beauty of the soul or intellectual compatibility. Maybe I'd been captivated by a story. Yes, I'd been captivated by a story, by a culture, by a history; can a person be smitten by a story? Clearly it does happen, I told myself. My desire to find Meleknaz throbbed like a toothache that occasionally made itself felt but that was always there. If I possessed Mesopotamian beliefs, I suppose I would have thought myself under the influence of Satan. I wondered if I should hang romaine lettuce on the door of the small apartment in Cihangir I had moved to after leaving my house to my ex-wife. Should I paint the brown door blue? If I went and did that one day, how would my neighbors and the doorman react? Especially to the lettuce! Would they call the police and say this journalist had gone mad? I tried to entertain myself with thoughts like this. I tried to make fun of myself, but somehow it didn't work. I couldn't pull out this passion that had put its roots into me like a poisonous vine.

Meleknaz and the blind baby were in Istanbul, but how was I to find them amid the confusion of fifteen million people? I pressured Aysel to tell me which friend Hussein had sent Meleknaz to. Did she have an address, a telephone number, even a first name? But she didn't know, she had no idea. I was at a dead end; I couldn't find a single clue. Then something interesting occurred to me. Perhaps I could find Meleknaz through Nergis. The baby needed medical care, and looking for a blind baby named Nergis might be easier than looking for Meleknaz. Where could the baby be? If she was in someone's home, it would be difficult, but there were other places I might find her. There were hospitals, orphanages, refugee shelters, and so forth... Nergis might be in a place like this, and she might have been brought to any doctor for treatment.

I decided to ask Nihal. She was familiar with the world of medical establishments; you know how every week there's a new plant with miraculous properties? She's one of the people who writes those articles. For a time I went back and forth between being glad I asked and regretting that I asked. Because in the bedlam of Istanbul there were so many such places that my task seemed impossible. In spite of this I didn't give up, and every evening I'd leave the newspaper and go home and read everything I could about the subject on the internet. I typed in the keywords and the names and searched and searched. Blind baby, refugee baby Nergis, Syrian Meleknaz, orphanage, hospital, eye clinics, opticians, shelters. I tried everything that came to mind; I was desperately looking for the end of a thread so that I could unravel this tangled ball.

Meanwhile I'd done everything my ex-wife wanted. I'd signed all the papers, and she would never again be part of my life. The shadow of that ambitious woman who thought only of career and property and who wanted so much to be Western would not fall on the pure, deep passion I had for Meleknaz's story. I had no patience left with this erroneous and immoral age, in which consumers were more valued than producers. I'd changed; Mardin had changed me. I couldn't stand hearing people talk about where to get the best sushi in Istanbul while people were suffering so much. When I saw these "plaza people" like my ex-wife—and there were so many of them, who struggle to consume and appear more Western in order to gain value—I couldn't help thinking of that little girl lying under a pile of rocks on Mount Shingal, now probably long since torn apart by animals.

I understood Hussein, I understood my childhood friend whose behavior I'd been surprised by when I heard about it in Mardin. I was slowly becoming like him. It was as if Hussein had opened my eyes and shown me the dementia of a schizophrenic nation with its mind in the West and its heart in the East, its citizens' uneasy personalities that lacked confidence and struggled to seem different from what they were by using foreign words and consuming foreign goods.

I could only fall asleep at night by holding the handkerchief with the black-and-red Peacock Angel embroidered on the corner. The mystery and deep pain of the East was drawing me into its dark vortex. I was swirling into the depths, becoming more like Hussein as I wandered after Meleknaz. This was something like falling in love with Mesopotamia on account of a girl I'd never seen. This had nothing to do with the concept of *harese* that Uncle Fuat had talked about. It had to do with love, legend, and magic being deeper in the East. The Arabs called the yearning of love *garam*. For love itself they had a word that meant the winding of a vine, which is perhaps more apt for yearning. Or at least I thought so, because I was caught up in the ecstasy of falling in love with an illusion. The handkerchief was soft, it smelled nice, and it had embroidered edges. Who knew where or when some girl had embroidered it? Which girl's delicate hands had embroidered that Peacock Angel? What had happened to those girls? If I talked about these girls to my ex-wife, would she understand at all? Would she be able to perceive that this handkerchief was as valuable as the most expensive European brand? Before falling asleep I would remember these two lines from Nazim Hikmet: *I come from the East / I come shouting about the revolt of the East.*

I'm an Easterner, I thought, I cast aside my years of Western education, of struggling to possess a European or American lifestyle, as if they were worn-out socks. I'm an Easterner, and for days I repeated to myself that I'd drunk the water of the East, that I came from the land of legends. I began thinking about relatives I hadn't thought of for years, the people who'd scattered to Ankara and Izmir: aunts, uncles, and cousins I hadn't seen in so long. If only, I thought, my father hadn't sent me to that boarding school in Istanbul, if only I hadn't become so alienated, if only I hadn't wasted so many years trying to be a Westerner, if only I'd been like Mehmet, if only I'd stayed in Mardin as he did and rested my back against a great plane tree. I would have had more self-confidence, I would have avoided seeming like a Westerner to Easterners, and seeming to Westerners like an Easterner who'd become alienated from his own people and lost his identity. This was all fantasy, of course. I had no choice but to carry this complicated identity.

Of course what I called the East wasn't the real East, but a fairy tale, and Meleknaz had come to symbolize this: Lalish, the magnificent caliphs of Baghdad, golden palaces, desert prophets who shook the earth, Lahore shawls, silk, daggers studded with emeralds and rubies, Sinbad in the belly of a fish, Firdawsī, Hafiz, Saadi, Imru' al-Qais. a more intricate version of *A Thousand and One Nights* was fluttering in my mind, and all of this was bound to an image of a delicate girl I'd never seen.

There was no chance I could have found her on my own, but thankfully the capable Nihal found the child in the end. She found out where Syrian refugee babies stayed, especially those who were sick, and she'd asked if there was a blind baby there. Apparently there weren't many babies who fit that description. One Saturday we went to an orphanage (it was called "The House of Love," yes, seriously, "The House of Love") on the pretext of conducting an interview, and I saw Nergis, whose eyes were clouded over. Nergis, who was born on Mount Shingal, who'd had to share her mother's milk with both Zilan and her mother. She was sucking on a pacifier; she seemed like a symbol of innocence created specially to reveal the dangers of the world. I felt strange when I saw her, as if what I'd read in a fairy tale, about a baby being born among the dead, had come to life. I'd listened to Zilan as if she were relating a strange Eastern fairy tale in which bloodstained angel feathers were flying about, but that baby, that baby... Unfortunately, she didn't come from the land of fairy tales. This baby who lived in darkness, who'd never seen Shingal, or her mother's face, or the refugee camp, or Hussein, or Aunt Adviye's house, or Istanbul, or the House of Love, lay there quietly, motionless, with dimples like rosebuds forming as she sucked on her pacifier. She's a very well-behaved child, they said, she never cries. We asked if she'd seen a doctor. They said yes, but there weren't any results yet. To tell the truth, I got the feeling that the staff there weren't going to a lot of trouble to get treatment for her. We asked if we could take her to an eye clinic. They said no, it was strictly forbidden for anyone to take children out of there—only her mother could take her. That's when my heart started beating. I tried to suppress my excitement and disguise my curiosity. I said that I wanted to learn that baby's story: who was her mother (meanwhile I also asked about her father), where were her parents, why did this happen to the baby, could I get their names and addresses? The staff member we talked to must have been a stickler for the rules. she said that this was "absolutely impossible." It was forbidden for outsiders to make contact with the families—it was absolutely, absolutely, forbidden. It was clear that this plump, middle-aged woman was fond of the word "absolutely." Fine, I said, if I were to leave a letter for these people whose names I don't know, would you be able to give it to them? If they're willing, would they be allowed to get in touch with me? I felt I would explode if the woman said "absolutely" again, but amazingly, she didn't. On the contrary, she said that this wasn't against the rules. She couldn't give me the mother's name, but she could deliver a letter to her, and what happened after that was none of her business. The baby's mother could decide for herself if she wanted to talk to me. Nihal said, "You mentioned the mother, does the baby have a father?" No, said the woman, or rather, I don't know, the mother comes to see the baby once a week. I asked why the baby didn't live with her mother. The woman saw no problem with telling me. She said the young woman was working as a live-in housekeeper, and she didn't have a home of her own; that's why she couldn't have the baby with her. I remember thinking that at this rate, the baby was never going to get treatment, and even if it was possible to restore her eyesight it wasn't going to happen. Because something like that would take money, private clinics: how could a government orphanage undertake that?

Dear Meleknaz,

You don't know me, but I'm a close friend of Hussein's. I would like to see you and tell you some things I think you need to know. I also have something that belongs to you. If you agree to meet me, please give a note with a time and a place to the person who delivered this letter.

This was the first letter I wrote to Meleknaz in Arabic, and I had a bit of trouble with it. The woman, who I felt was beginning to soften toward me, said she would give the letter to the baby's mother when she came. "If she wants to write anything to me, here's my card, it has my address, phone number, and email." She promised to get the note to Meleknaz right away.

Then I waited. I checked my messages and emails constantly every day, but there was nothing. Then, eight days later, a message made my heart jump for joy.

"The Akın cafe in Aksaray, Sunday at three o'clock."

I think that because she worked every day, and she'd chosen Sunday as her day off, she must have been going to visit the orphanage on Sundays too. The nurse had said she came once a week to see the baby.

As others had said, the first thing that struck me about her was her eyes; black, slightly slanted, looking straight at you, never glancing away. Her eyes had a strange attraction, like a magnetic field. When I sat across from her I told her that I felt as if I knew her. Everyone had talked so much about her, that even though this was our first meeting I felt I knew her. I kept talking—I felt as if I had to talk to break the silence between us, as if this was my duty. As you might have guessed, she didn't say anything, she just looked at me. She was the strong one, she had the right to remain silent. For my part, I was trying to ingratiate myself. In whatever manner the unspoken contract between two people begins, it continues that way. This is how our roles are handed out to us.

"I don't want compassion, I don't need anyone to feel sorry for me, compassion is a part of cruelty. Compassion can't be a balm for cruelty."

She didn't say this aloud, but her eyes said it. I was thinking about the nights on Mount Shingal: dark, moonless nights, flickering stars bound to the mountain with ropes. Never in my life had I seen—how can I put it, it wasn't hatred, it wasn't defiance (I was trying to find a word to describe what her eyes said), it wasn't resentment either, perhaps *indifference*. Indifferent glances that said, "I don't need your compassion, I don't need anyone's compassion." If this young woman with long black hair and a thin face had shouted this, it wouldn't have been more effective. She didn't say a thing, she just looked, and this gave me a strange uneasiness. Indifferent, I thought, yes, she's indifferent, she's not interested. It was as if she wasn't in this world, a living person wouldn't stare so far into the distance. Words such as *arrogance, defiance, reproach, offense, hopelessness, pain, pleading, chagrin, lovelessness, umbrage, coldness, rebuke,* and *injury* weren't sufficient to explain the look in her eyes. Indeed the word *pain* wasn't at all right. I'd seen a bit of this in Zilan's eyes as well; a look that contained no emotion, no expectation; a look that carried nothing, that had gone past both delight and pain. With Meleknaz this look was more intense, deeper, more mysterious. As if she wanted to say, "Go ahead and say what you want to say so we can get this over with."

I was struggling to convince the girl. I said I would bring her no harm, I was Hussein's friend, we'd been friends since childhood: I went to Mardin, I learned about what happened to you, I saw Aunt Adviye and Aysel, I spoke to your sheikh, I learned about your religion, I respect the Peacock Angel. And then I saw Zilan, your friend Zilan, I heard about what happened to Nergis. I went to the Deyrulzafaran monastery, I talked to the priest. That is, until today I've been following traces of you, I wanted to find you, to see you, I was curious. I've been thinking for months about who this Meleknaz is, and now here we are, but you won't talk to me.

She listened to what I was saying to her in Arabic. Her lips were sealed, and there wasn't even the slightest movement on her face. I wanted to tell her that perhaps she was right: Zilan was like you too, I'm someone who doesn't understand what it means to move beyond pain. You people have moved beyond a threshold, you're beyond good and evil, beyond pain. We are unable to understand this, but

I beg you to give me the opportunity to understand this. I'm telling you that I'm Hussein's friend, *his best friend, since we were five years old*. (I was flat-out lying, or rather I was misleading her by mixing fact and fiction.) I asked her if she knew about what had happened to Hussein.

Please excuse me if I keep saying the same things over and over again; put it down to my intoxication with the East. In a sneaky rain that turned everything and everyone gray, at a plastic table in a cafe in Istanbul, the smell of wet coats mixing with the smell of coffee, I tried to express my gratitude to her for agreeing to meet me. I was trying to convince this black-eyed, thin-faced girl to tell me everything. I can help you, I said, maybe I can help you. How, she asked, in a cold, distant voice. Can you bring Hussein back, can you bring Nergis back, can you bring the bodies rotting under the earth back to life?

I wanted to tell her that I was Hussein now, that she should accept me as Hussein, that I was there to replace him, but I didn't say this. Instead I said no, I wasn't a prophet, I couldn't resurrect anyone. Then keep quiet, she said. She stood, taking the old, worn-out bag she'd hung on her chair. She moved with the litheness of youth, but the slump of her delicate shoulders revealed the hopelessness within her.

I stood, and as she walked toward the door I went after her. I asked her to stop, to please stop. She heard me, but the way she shook the silky black hair that fell over her shoulders told me that I wasn't going to be able to get through to her.

She opened the frosted glass door of the cafe and stepped into the misty rain, letting go of the swinging door. I caught the door before it hit me in the face and tried to catch up to her. She was walking quickly. The light rain had now become a downpour. I practically ran to catch up to her. Of course I can't change what happened, I said, but I can help you. it's too difficult for you to carry this burden alone, and I don't think you're going to make it. But I can help you, I really can.

I was running as I said this. The rain had plastered her hair to her left temple, and I could see her profile. She didn't say anything to me. She didn't answer, she ignored me. She looked straight ahead as she walked, and I thought, may all of the Mesopotamian gods forgive me, she was very beautiful, the essence of this woman for whom Hussein had burned himself to ashes. As always, the combination of a woman's will and her beauty created a strange ache in me. For a while I ran alongside her, saying meaningless and embarrassing things. Fine, I said, it's clear I can't convince you to talk to me, please call me if you ever need anything, please, please, please, please. As my last "please" faded into the misty air, it was as if it was I who was in difficult circumstances. I felt defeated in the face of her powerful character. I stood watching her walk away along the avenue in the mist, defeated in a clash of wills. I suddenly thought that I was losing her. I thought of the burning misery I would feel after I parted from her, how once again I would feel as if my heart was being carved out by a sharp instrument. I called out once more in hopelessness, "Meleknaz, please stop, there's more I have to tell you, and I have something that belongs to you." She didn't hear me, and I watched her walk off into the distance.

Then it occurred to me to follow her. I supposed something like this would make her angry, but there was no other way I could make contact with her. Meleknaz was some distance ahead of me, I started to follow her, taking care not to let her catch on. I walked along under the awnings of closed shops. I didn't really expect her to do so, but I wanted to be able to hide in a doorway if she suddenly turned around. As I watched the girl walk quickly like a desert gazelle, I thought what pride, what stubbornness, what defiance. Though she was wearing a worn-out gray raincoat that someone had probably given her out of charity and a pair of very worn-out shoes, her feet were probably getting wet in this rain. Perhaps for someone who had lost everything, honor was the only remaining shelter, the last thing she possessed. I knew that sooner or later the girl was going to enter a building, the place where she worked. I'd learned at the orphanage that she worked as a live-in housekeeper.

And now I was going to find out where that house was, I would soon see the house where Meleknaz worked. I had no idea what I was going to do after that, but if I didn't find that house, Meleknaz would be lost to me forever. My search for Meleknaz, my adventure of tracking her down, would end on a middle-class street in front of a middle-class apartment building.

After Meleknaz went inside, I passed in front of the building. There was a dirty blue sign: I saw the number 18. Blue, I said to myself, a blue sign, how could that be? How could Meleknaz stand that? Fine, I thought later, but there's blue everywhere in Istanbul, in every corner, in every letter, every street sign. And I, a faceless journalist in this enormous city, was trying to save my soul by forcing help on someone who didn't want it. As streams of rainwater ran down the back of my neck like wet worms, I pitied poor Ibrahim.

I'd thought that when I saw Meleknaz my curiosity would diminish a bit, that I'd be free of my obsessions, but it was exactly the opposite. It seemed as if the process of becoming Hussein, the sense that I felt the same things as Hussein, only became stronger. Everyone at the newspaper noticed how distracted I was on Monday. Some people asked whether or not I was ill, others secretly made fun of me. We'd all become accustomed to this thorny, loveless environment, we'd all long since learned the realities that killed the souls of the plaza people and turned them into robots. Unless you wore the invisible armor of indifference, like the metal armor of knights in the Middle Ages, there was no chance of finding shelter around here. In the beginning, when a friend saw how shaken I was by this milieu, he said everyone had an umbrella to protect themselves, but you don't have one: open your umbrella as soon as possible, because this rain is never going to stop. I thought I'd learned to keep my umbrella open and wear my armor, but in fact I hadn't, until a Meleknaz appeared and shook me, carved my heart out and turned my world upside down. Upside down. I thought that this was the best way to describe the situation. Nothing else quite described it.

For days I smelled that handkerchief. I fell asleep stroking my face with it. For days I walked down that street, past that building, I writhed with the desire to see Meleknaz and tell her that I was Hussein. I wanted to tell her to replace Hussein with me: "There's no need for you to work as a servant. I have a home, it's yours, move into my home. Nergis can come too, we'll bring the baby to the best doctors in Istanbul; Zilan can come too." But I had no chance to say these things to her; I couldn't even see her. And I was certain that if I did see her she would look at me once again with those indifferent eyes. She wouldn't even feel the need to say that she didn't require anything from me; that look would pierce me. Being a servant didn't hurt her pride, but compassion wounded her. She didn't want compassion. She'd made up her mind about humanity; she'd closed herself off so thoroughly that she wouldn't allow even the smallest beam of light into the pitch darkness in which she sat. She looked like someone who drew strength from hopelessness, but the moment she allowed this to be shaken she would collapse. So this is what happens when all of your confidence in humanity is completely destroyed, a darkness in which the doors and windows of hope were firmly shut, an iron gate that would no longer open for anyone... The girls from Lalish had learned this lesson from life. The best way to avoid the danger of hoping again, and then collapsing again, like a sea creature retreating into its shell. Fine, but how was I going to get into that shell?

I sat down and wrote her a letter, a short letter:

I have something of yours that might be important to you, I wasn't able to give it to you, so I still have it. Every Sunday I'll wait for you at the same time and the same place.

I wrote "Ms. Meleknaz" on the envelope and went to that apartment building in Aksaray. I rang the doorman's bell, and when a man asked "Who is it?" through the intercom, I shouted that I wanted to deliver a letter. When a man with a thin moustache came out, I asked whether or not he knew Meleknaz. At first he frowned as if he didn't know who I was talking about. I told him she was a Syrian refugee. "Ha," he said, "do you mean that Syrian maid? I was confused when you called her Meleknaz. We call her Melek—she works at number 4." I asked him if he would deliver the letter; it was from a relative. The man agreed, he said it was a good deed to help these miserable people: "That poor girl is so quiet. Sometimes she mops the stairs in the building to help me out." He asked me if I wanted to see her. I said no, thank you, it's enough if you just give her the letter.

After that, the days of waiting began; I got through the week with hopes that she would come that Sunday. On Sundays I waited impatiently for the time to pass until it was three o'clock.

On the first Sunday, I wrapped the handkerchief in some nice wrapping paper and put it in my pocket. Then I went to the cafe and sat at the same table. Meleknaz didn't come. I waited until four thirty, and then, feeling hopeless, I got up and went home. I took the handkerchief out of the wrapping paper and put it on my pillow. I was torn apart about Meleknaz, but I was also frightened of her. Just as you can't try to comfort a tiger who's fallen into a trap and been mortally wounded, no matter how much you might want to, you can't bandage those wounds. I couldn't approach Meleknaz for the same reason. It was like seeing a cat in pain who swipes its claws at you thinking you too will harm it. There's nothing you can do but watch helplessly.

The following Sunday I once again wrapped the handkerchief in gift paper, and at three o'clock I once again went to the cafe and sat at the same table. She didn't come. She didn't come the following Sunday either, or the Sunday after that. Out of stubbornness, I kept going every Sunday. On the fifth Sunday I got my reward. As I sat hopelessly at the table, I saw her pass the cafe, frowning and with a sullen expression. When I saw her open the door and walk in my heart leapt; I could hear my racing pulse. I swelled with delight, as if this was the greatest favor anyone had ever done me. I jumped to my feet with a smile, I put out my hand but she didn't shake it. She sat without changing the expression on her face, and she didn't say anything. I told her I had something of hers, but just then the waiter came to take our orders, Meleknaz asked for water. I ordered water for her, coffee for myself, and I asked for some cake as well. I was trying to be unnecessarily gracious to someone who had survived on her own milk on a mountain. She would look down on me for this, but so what? Her disdain wasn't for me, it was for the entire human race. I put the gift-wrapped package on the table (the wrapping paper was red, not blue, of course). What is this, she asked. Something that belongs to you, I said, please open it. She opened it reluctantly, but the moment she saw the handkerchief, I saw her frozen expression change for the first time. She took the handkerchief, turned it over several times, and then asked me where I'd found it. I told her I'd found it in the sun temple. She asked me if I'd gone there, and I said yes, I followed your traces wherever I could. She asked me why, and I said I didn't know: "I really don't know why but you've become the center of my life. I kept trying to find you, I kept trying to find an angel."

"You don't even know me," she said.

I said I did know her, I thought I knew her.

"But I don't know you," she said.

"I'm struggling to let you know me," I said. Meanwhile the young waiter, who knew me very well by now, brought the water, the coffee, and the cake. I kept talking in the best Arabic I could summon. I said I knew about what had happened to her and to her people; she looked at me with a mocking expression, I told her I was trying to understand. I asked her to allow me to become closer to her, I wanted to try to show her that not everyone in the world was evil.

To tell the truth, what I was saying sounded strange to me. While I was trying to have a personal conversation with Meleknaz, it sounded as if I was delivering a sermon on good and evil in people. Anyway, Meleknaz brought me to my senses. She asked me why I was telling her all these things. I remained silent for a while; I really wondered why I was saying these things. Then I looked into her eyes and said, "Because I want to help you, Meleknaz." I said this with a courage that surprised even me: "Please don't misunderstand, it's more myself I want to help than you. I want to remember that I'm a human being. I want to get treatment for Nergis. I feel a deep disquiet, a disquiet that's killing me slowly."

I said a few other similar confused things. I talked nonsense without realizing that it's much more difficult to defeat mistrust that it is to deal with hostility. I talked so much that in the end I got the feeling that I might have confused her a bit, that she might be beginning to wonder. I thought that for a moment, a brief moment, she was thinking about trusting me, that a small chink may have opened in the wall of steel that surrounded her.

She suddenly took the handkerchief and got up. She thanked me, and I walked her to the door. I said I would continue to go there every Sunday at the same time. Then I added, I've been deprived of my only consolation, your handkerchief, but I believe that you'll come one day, you'll come one Sunday. Help me, help me, help me!

She left without saying anything. For years I'd thought about how surprised I was by the strength that some women have: Where do they get this confidence, stubbornness, and decisiveness? What's the source of their strength? Why were men so much weaker and miserable when it came to emotions? Was it a superiority of the soul to balance men's physical strength? I don't think I'd ever seen anyone, woman or man, who possessed the kind of pride this girl did. If she was responding to me this way, why was she willing to let Hussein take her out of the camp? I knew that the answer to this question was especially important, but I had no idea how to begin untying this knot. I thought about Mardin, about what I'd heard people tell me about Hussein, about what I'd heard in the camp. What was it that made the difference? Then I thought of something: Was it compassion that made her angry? She withstood the people who treated her badly, but she was angered by people who showed her compassion. Hussein hadn't shown Meleknaz any special compassion. He was already working at the camp, and he was struggling to help all of the refugees: it wasn't a matter of any special compassion for Meleknaz, but he'd fallen in love with her. Of course that wasn't something that would wound the girl's pride. On the contrary, those beautiful poems must have made her feel like she was being worshipped.

I thought that in the end I'd reached the truth: compassion is a sharp sword—the one showing compassion grips the hilt, but it wounds the other person. Didn't the Prophet say that the hand that gives is superior to the hand that receives? Isn't this why they received the angel from America so coldly? Isn't this why they don't trust

Christian compassion? There was a story my father told me as I child that hadn't meant anything to me. The Caliph Ali was told that someone or other was saying slanderous things behind his back. He said he was surprised, because he'd never done that person a good deed.

I suppose I'd begun to understand what that meant. The man couldn't bear the weight of that good deed, so he put Ali down. Would you have wanted people to treat you with compassion at the newspaper, I asked myself. Would you have wanted them to feel sorry for you, to think that you were miserable? Was the passion I'd begun to feel even before I saw Meleknaz's face in fact a struggle to prove I was a good person? Was it an attempt to give meaning to a life that had been shaken, alienated, and stripped of every kind of value? Insisting on doing good to someone who didn't want it was nonsense, I knew that, or to tell the truth I couldn't know, I wasn't in a state to answer that question. I just wanted to be close to Meleknaz's noble stance, to her pride. For me she wasn't someone to pity. Her pride raised her to such heights that I couldn't even dream about touching her as I would in an ordinary relationship between a man and a woman. Thoughts of kissing those sealed lips, of seeing her naked, of feeling the warmth of her skin, were so distant they didn't even enter my dreams.

I spent a large part of that week in the secondhand book market. I set out on a mysterious journey in the bookstalls under those domes, among dusty books with yellowed pages, it was as if each of those quiet, offended books contained a secret. I stroked those beautiful bindings, and then I found the treasure I was seeking; the Mu'allaqat of Imru' al-Qais. The greatest of the seven poets whose poems were hung in the sacred Kaaba in the period before Islam. Words as sacred and moving as those found in the Black Stone in the temple Abraham built. Otherwise why would they have been hung on the wall of that most sacred place of pilgrimage? This poet's enchanting verses, which were once believed to have been taken from the invisible world, took wing and flew to me and the future from fifteen hundred years ago. They would bring me burning love poems that would both save my identity and convince Meleknaz. It if was true that in the East everything began with words, then I had to seize the reins of the horse of words. I had to be like Hussein. Indeed I had to become Hussein.

It was very strange to see myself as Hussein in my dreams, but that's the way it was.

One evening, I don't know whether my ecstatic mind was spinning more from the wine or from Imru' al-Qais, I emulated this ancient Arabic poem and wrote these lines:

In the name of the falling night
In the name of the westerly breeze
In the name of Mount Shingal
In the name of the nightingale that warbles at the rose
I am a slave who wishes not for freedom.

The following Sunday I went to the cafe again. I thought of her and wrote poetry, I wrote poetry and thought of her.

One Sunday you'll come, I said, I'll wait forever. The disquiet within me didn't pass, and neither did the feeling I had that I was doing something wrong. I woke in the night and wondered whether all of this was just to protect my dead childhood friend's fiancée. And what were all these love poems about?

Two weeks later, a strange thing happened, I ripped up and threw away all of the poems I'd written in emulation of Hussein. They seemed ridiculous to me; it was all needless prattle. My goal wasn't to suffer from love, it was something else altogether. I didn't know quite what it was, I couldn't put a name to it, but I was still certain it was something completely different. After ripping up and throwing away all of those pages covered in poetry, I felt relieved. I felt I'd turned back from the wrong path: even if I hadn't found the right path, at least I was no longer on what was certainly the wrong path. "Help me, Meleknaz," I said, "help me find the right path, help me by allowing me to help you, help me to come to value myself, help me to save this worthless man who's flailing about." It was as if my mother, my father, my country, and my vanished childhood were bound to the dreamlike image of this thin girl.

I continued to sit at the plastic table at the cafe every Sunday at three. Meleknaz didn't come, and the young waiter would give me a sad look, saying "It seems she didn't come again today." I ignored his efforts to give me something on the house. I just drank my tea and then went home. I went the following Sunday, she didn't come, and so forth . . . I'm still going.

I repeat this verse to myself, *Wait there cafe, even if she hasn't come, I still have hope.*

I was certain she would come one Sunday.

I finished this book with those words. I thought that this traumatic story that had begun when I received news of Hussein's death was over. But it seems all of that was just a beginning. I realized this a month later. One morning, news came from the agencies that hundreds of Ezidi who'd come from Mardin and Diyarbakır had tried to cross into Bulgaria and had been turned back at the border, and that they were waiting in misery by the side of the highway. Among the dozens of people at the newspaper, this news concerned me most. It was as if it was my own relatives who were waiting there.

I asked the chief editor for a car and a news photographer. He agreed, and I set out for the border city of Edirne. It was at most a two-hour drive from Istanbul. We took the TEM highway, the road that connects us to Europe. About five or six kilometers out of Edirne, we saw the rural police gathered by the side of the road. They stood there in their khaki uniforms, their rifles glinting in the sunlight. They were facing a crowd of men, women, and children who were sitting on the ground on pieces of cardboard or newspaper. It was a strange sight, as if the people who had been living in tents in the camp in Mardin had been brought here on flying carpets; the same hopelessness, the same waiting, the same misery. They'd set out from Mardin in five buses, but they'd been stopped five kilometers from the border. Europe didn't want them. They couldn't stand to see their faces, and they were doing everything they could to keep them from crossing the border. We knew that this was why they'd put pressure on Turkey. They were being prevented from getting to the border or dispersing into the city. They weren't allowing them to do anything except sit there on the wet ground.

We showed the police sergeant our press cards and got through the perimeter. We went in among the miserable Ezidi. Hakan started to take pictures, and no one paid any attention to him. When I saw a pale young woman with a baby in her arms, I said that's Meleknaz, there's another Meleknaz, and another one next to her. There were a lot of Meleknazes here: they were all here. Those who'd fled Mount Shingal, broken branches of the tree of humanity, those who'd escaped so many massacres, were here. Meleknaz wasn't here, but there were other Meleknazes here. There were Nergises and Zilans here, the innocents of the Peacock Angel were here. ISIS was behind them, and Europe was in front of them.

It seemed that in the end I'd found what it was I was supposed to do. You stop and take a rest, Peacock Angel, I said, perhaps you, like the god of the Torah, were wearied after creating the world in six days. On the first day you created light and darkness, day and night. On the second day you made the sky, and then you created the land, the sea, the grasses, the plants, the seeds and the fruit. On the fourth day it was time for the sun, the moon, and the stars. On the fifth day you filled the earth with all kinds of creatures, you created humankind in your own image to dominate the earth, and you divided them into men and women. Then you looked at what you'd created and said that it was good. On the sixth day you created all of the elements to complete the sky and the earth. On the seventh day your work was finished, and you withdrew to rest; perhaps the seventh day wasn't over yet, because the screams of the innocent sufferers don't reach you and everything is not good.

I turned on my phone's voice recorder, knelt next to the Meleknaz who was breastfeeding her baby, and began asking my questions...